Joseph H McCullagh

The Sunday-School Man of the South

A sketch of the life and labors of the Rev. John McCullagh

Joseph H McCullagh

The Sunday-School Man of the South
A sketch of the life and labors of the Rev. John McCullagh

ISBN/EAN: 9783337097509

Printed in Europe, USA, Canada, Australia, Japan

Cover: Foto ©Raphael Reischuk / pixelio.de

More available books at **www.hansebooks.com**

"THE SUNDAY-SCHOOL MAN OF THE SOUTH."

A SKETCH OF THE LIFE AND LABORS

OF THE

REV. JOHN McCULLAGH.

BY THE

REV. JOSEPH H. McCULLAGH.

WITH AN INTRODUCTION BY THE

REV. EDWIN W. RICE, D.D.

———

PHILADELPHIA

THE AMERICAN SUNDAY-SCHOOL UNION,

1122 CHESTNUT STREET.

NEW YORK: 8 AND 10 BIBLE HOUSE.

1889.

DEDICATION.

TO THE MANY THOUSANDS OF MY FATHER'S BELOVED FRIENDS
THROUGHOUT THIS UNION, FROM THE LITTLE ONES IN
SUNDAY-SCHOOLS TO THE VENERABLE SAINTS OF FOUR-
SCORE YEARS, WHO HAVE OFTEN LISTENED WITH
PLEASURE TO THE STIRRING APPEALS FROM
THE VOICE THAT IS NOW SILENT, AND WHO,
BY THEIR KIND WORDS OF CHEER AND
GENEROUS CONTRIBUTIONS TO THE
GREAT CAUSE TO WHICH HE
DEVOTED HIS LIFE,
MADE THE OLD MISSIONARY'S HEART REJOICE,
AND HIS LIFE ONE OF TRIUMPH,

This Volume

IS AFFECTIONATELY DEDICATED

BY THE AUTHOR.

INTRODUCTION.

Any well-written biography of a good person inspires the living to fill their lives with good deeds. If, as Carlyle says, "the history of what man has accomplished in this world is at bottom the history of the great men who have worked here," then this little book is no unimportant contribution to the history of the American people in the South; for those who occupy high public offices are not the only great men of a nation. "Given a great soul open to the divine significance of life," and you will have a person fit to speak and to do great things. In a high or a humble sphere such a soul will become, nay is, one of the world's great men.

Hence every true reform and every important movement develops great souls. They are the world's heroes; recognized in their period and place, and justly honored for their achievements. To this noble army of confessors and great men John McCullagh belonged. Good biographies of such men are among the most instructive and valuable works in Christian literature. A better class of books for Sunday-school libraries and for the home is not to be found.

This unpretending yet admirable sketch of the "Sunday-school Man of the South" will be read with avidity by thousands who have been stirred by his eloquent appeals, and by thousands of others who have been blessed by his indefatigable labors. The consecrated

Scotch lad, upon whose head the beloved Thomas Chalmers kindly laid his hand, accompanying it with thoughtful counsel, was ever after inspired with a good measure of the same fiery zeal that filled the heart of the greatest of modern Scotch preachers. Scotch perseverance, animated by such zeal, enabled McCullagh to sweep everything before him.

It is a difficult task to write a just and interesting biography; but this delicate work has been performed with rare discrimination, excellent taste and graphic conciseness by the son, the Rev. Joseph H. McCullagh, now gracefully wearing the mantle and vigorously carrying forward the work dear to his father's heart. The fragrance of such a consecrated life as John McCullagh's is sweet: it deserves to be held in remembrance, as it long will be, south and north, and may cheer many a discouraged soul, by the help of God, to do a heroic work for the Master, in the face of adverse fortune, and in a strange land.

Edwin W. Rice.

Philadelphia, July 10, 1889.

CONTENTS.

CHAPTER IX.

CHAPTER X.

CHAPTER XI.

CHAPTER XII.

CHAPTER XX.

THE SUNDAY-SCHOOL MAN
OF THE SOUTH.

CHAPTER I.

EARLY LIFE.

MANY years ago, a little boy in Scotland lay suffering with brain fever. His mother was a widow, and he was now her only son. Thrice already had she been called to mourn, like "Rachel weeping *for* her children, and would not be comforted, because they are not." According to the custom of that time, the physician was bleeding the little sufferer, to reduce the fever; and while feeling the pulse, which was beating weaker and weaker, his face was grave and troubled. The mother was looking on with anguish and despair.

"John," said the physician, "has the pain left you?"

"Yes, sir; the moment you spoke it stopped."

15

"Thank God, you will recover. The crisis is past."

These words from the doctor brought sunshine to the mother's heart and face. This boy, whose life had been quivering in a balance, was John McCullagh.

He was born near Glasgow, Scotland, October 31, 1811, being the youngest of four children. His brother Joseph, and two sisters, died quite early in life. His father died when John was very young. It was with joy like unto that of the Shunammite woman, whose son was raised from the dead by Elisha, that this afflicted Scottish mother heard her son would recover.

She was a woman of great strength of character and of deep religious convictions. When her son was restored to health, she bent all her energies to train him in a godly and pious manner. The Bible, the Confession of Faith and Shorter Catechism were her text-books. Faith, prayer and holy living were her methods of teaching. The pupil was an apt scholar, having a bright mind and a remarkable memory. Chapter after chapter from God's word was

thoroughly learned. The Psalms of David in
metre, such as are used in the Scottish
churches, were memorized. These he never
forgot; and when over seventy years of age he
could sit and repeat by the hour, with all the
quaint sweetness of the Scotch brogue, these
beautiful Psalms and truths of God which he
had learned at his mother's knee.

While the boy was quite young, the noted
Rev. Dr. Thomas Chalmers came to Glasgow,
as pastor of the Tron Church, and commenced
his wonderful work of Sabbath-school and
church extension in the destitute portions of
that city. John McCullagh attended Dr. Chalmers' Sabbath-school in Glasgow, and afterwards in Edinburgh. He was a faithful and
diligent scholar, and often spoke of the day
when Dr. Chalmers took him by the hand and
led him out before the Sunday-school and
praised him for memorizing Bible verses. The
love and admiration which John McCullagh
had for Dr. Thomas Chalmers became one of
the controlling influences of his life. It was
from Chalmers' work that he grasped the idea,
in after years, that Sabbath-school work among

2

the poor and destitute was the greatest door open for Christian activity; Chalmers having said, "I see more good results from my Sabbath-school in Kilmany than from all my other work." It would be an interesting study to trace out the power and influence of Dr. Chalmers' example on the life of John McCullagh. The same fire that burned in the heart of the Nestor of Scotch preachers was communicated to the breast of his Sabbath-school scholar, and borne by him through the forests of America.

When a young man, he entered the University of Glasgow. Geometry and the higher mathematics had especial attractions for him. Surveying, civil engineering and astronomy were also favorite studies. Owing to failing health, he was compelled to suspend his studies for several years. During this time he was connected with a commission house, and travelled for it through the north of Ireland and west of Scotland. This active life having benefited him, he returned to the university to complete his education.

About this time his mother died. His affectionate, tender heart always treasured her precious memory as sacred; and even during his last days, when speaking of her, there was a peculiar tenderness and pathos in his tone.

Just before completing his theological studies, another trial of a different nature befell him. He had inherited quite a handsome property, but had been induced to indorse for some friends; their enterprise failed and he had to pay the notes. This swept away his fortune in one day.

He now resolved to leave Scotland and go to America. His plan had been to devote himself to Sunday-school work in Great Britain, and he had organized Sabbath-schools among the colliers and fishermen in Scotland, and the Irish in Connaught; but America seemed to be the more promising field.

His family were all dead, and his fortune gone. He wished to leave the place of so many sorrowful and unpleasant associations, and go to a new world, and devote his life to the great work of training the young for Christ.

Before leaving Great Britain, he visited the Giant's Causeway and the Irish coast. One day, on this visit, he secured a gig to drive along the beautiful coast. Night overtook him before he returned. The way was lonesome, and there was no one in the vehicle except himself and the driver. Suddenly two men, armed with clubs, rushed out of the bushes and seized the horse by the bridle. "Highwaymen," said McCullagh to himself, "and I am unarmed!" But his courage did not fail; and rising, he shouted in a loud voice, "Let go that horse, or I will make you!" At the same time he snapped the spring of his umbrella twice, sharply. The larger man cried to his companion, "Run, Mike! that fellow has a pistol." In an instant they were gone, and he returned safely; but the adventure terminated the trip for sight-seeing.

CHAPTER II.

GOES TO AMERICA.

In the spring of 1834 he was ready to leave for New York. The last sermon he heard in England was by Dr. McNeill, a distinguished minister in Liverpool, from the text, "The Master is come, and calleth for thee" (John 11 : 28). The whole discourse seemed as if it had been specially prepared for him. It said to him in substance, "God, by his providence, has brought you to this point. The ship is in the harbor, ready to carry you over the sea. A great work is before you. Be of good courage, 'It is I, be not afraid.'"

He had secured passage in the Jane Walker, a strong new ship, which was to sail that week; but meeting some friends in Liverpool, who desired that he should remain some time with them, he went to the office of the owners and asked that his passage be changed to that of the Margaret, a brig belonging to the same owners, and which was to sail two weeks later.

"Yes, we will change you," said the agent, "if you will pay us a handsome bonus." "What! pay a bonus to be changed from a new ship to an old brig? I will do nothing of the kind; I will go on the Jane Walker."

The Margaret sailed two weeks later from an earthly port, but landed her passengers in eternity. Not a spar was found to tell how, when or where she was lost.

When he went on board the Jane Walker, the first thing that met his gaze was a young sailor lying on the deck in a state of beastly intoxication. The sailors were standing around laughing at him. One of them said, "Wait until the mate comes on board, and he will put that fellow ashore in a hurry." Mr. McCullagh looked at the unfortunate man, and saw that he had a fine, open face. He was moved with pity toward him, and said to one of the sailors, "He looks like a good fellow; you take hold of his feet and I will take his arms, and we will carry him off the deck."

They carried him below, and covered him with some old sails. The next day the ship was out at sea, and the young sailor had become sober. As he was walking on the deck the sailors pointed to Mr. McCullagh, and said to the young man, "That is the gentleman who saved your bacon."

The ship was fifty days in making the voyage. After getting within six hundred miles of New York, contrary winds arose, which, for three weeks, blew them steadily back toward Liverpool.

One night, on this voyage, while a storm was raging, a man went to the room where the casks of fresh water were kept. He left the key out which held them in place, so that the rolling of the vessel threw them out of position, and they were soon in such a condition that one half of the water supply was lost.

The next morning the order was, "Water rations cut down one half." Some days later this was again reduced, until a water famine threatened them in mid-ocean.

The young man whom Mr. McCullagh had befriended was placed in charge of the water supply. He told him he was now ready to repay him for his kindness, and that he would put a gallon jug full of water in his room every morning. The offer was accepted, and every day he went among the steerage passengers, a large number of whom were on board, and many of them sick, and held a glass of water to their parched lips. If he had given them gold and diamonds they could not have been more grateful. He said he had never appreciated what a blessing water was until then.

A Colonel Bailey, a blaspheming infidel, was on board. His horrid oaths shocked all who heard them. One night the ship was reported to be going down under the terrible sweep of the tempest. Colonel Bailey was in his room, praying very earnestly. A number of passengers gathered around his door to hear him. One of them said, " Why, he can out-pray a preacher."

The next day the sky was clear, and when the colonel was congratulated upon his gift in prayer, he swore that it was all a lie, he never prayed in his life. This convinced Mr. McCullagh that some infidels are cowards when danger is near.

After a long and stormy voyage the Jane Walker reached New York safely.

CHAPTER III.

It was with great joy that Mr. McCullagh first gazed on the New World, bathed in the glories of the rising sun. Here was to be the scene of his trials and triumphs; this people were to be his people, their God, his God. After landing he called to see Mr. Robert Carter, the noted book publisher, to whom he bore letters of introduction. From Mr. Carter he received much useful information about the points of difference between this country and Scotland.

While in the city he heard of The American Sunday-School Union, and pondered over the name. "American, that means national, not sectional; Sunday-School, that means spiritual, not secular; Union, that means united effort for Christ. I like everything about it. That name expresses my sentiments. I suppose they have experienced men to do the very kind of work I intend to perform. I am a raw recruit, and know nothing of this country, but I can be a volunteer. Without asking any pay from the society, I can help them in their grand work. I enlist in that cause for life."

He resolved that instead of becoming an ordained minister, where his influence would be local, he would devote himself to missionary work, and go to the war on his own charges. He reasoned thus: "While I have but little money I have good health, an education, and am a civil engineer. With these resources I can always make a living and have time to work for the Master. If I teach school I will be brought in contact with the young, and can have great influence over them. If Paul practiced the trade of tent-making in order to preach the gospel without charge, I have a good scriptural example for my model; and if this country is as vast and boundless as they tell me it is, and the population so widely scattered, there are thousands who never hear the preacher's voice. The church and Sunday-school societies cannot support all the men required to reach them. I will be a volunteer in the army of King Jesus, will bear my own expenses, and go where I think the most good can be done. I will unfurl the blood-stained banner of the Cross, and tell of his wondrous love to sinners."

On the following Sabbath he went to hear Rev. Dr. Gardiner Spring preach. This was the first sermon he heard in America. The text was, "Ye *are* my witnesses, saith the LORD" (Isaiah 43 : 10). The theme was personal work for Christ. One of the main points of the sermon was the importance of work in the Sunday-school. Mr. McCullagh was highly pleased and greatly edified by the discourse. "That is the true doctrine," he exclaimed; "that sounds like Dr. Chalmers."

After a short stay in New York city he went to Monticello, Sullivan county, New York. Here he was very kindly received by Rev. Dr. James Adams. The first sermon he heard from Dr. Adams was from the text, "Ye are our epistle written in our hearts, known and read of all men" (2 Corinthians 3 : 2), bringing out the great idea of Christian influence and the glory of Christian work. Dr. Adams cordially indorsed Mr. McCullagh's views of Sunday-school missionary labor, and often accompanied him on his missionary trips. To strengthen his views he read to him Dr. Archibald Alexander's opinion, as follows: "I have a favorite notion that this is a rich, uncultivated missionary field. There should be a class of preachers for children alone. If I were a young man I would, God willing, choose that field."

While living in Monticello, on one occasion he became involved in a discussion with a learned judge of that place, who was an Arian and a very subtle reasoner. The debate waxed warm, and a large company gathered around the disputants.

Finally, Mr. McCullagh said, "Judge, you have the advantage of me. You know what I believe, but I do not know what you believe."

"I believe the Bible."

"Do you believe the Bible?"

"Yes," he replied, "I believe the Bible."

"Well then, you are a lawyer and a judge; it is your business to make a very close study of words to ascertain their exact meaning, and to construe them strictly and accurately. Now then, if God, the great Father of us all, wished you and me and every one to believe that Jesus

Christ was divine, and in a way so clear that nobody could misunderstand it, will you please tell us, as a judge, what terms should be used to express the truth?"

"Well," replied the judge, "if God wished us to believe Jesus to be divine he would have said in the Bible, *He is the true God.*"

The auditors all agreed to the judge's statement, and thought the young Scotchman was cornered; but he quietly turned to the judge's daughter and said, "Miss A., will you please take your Bible and turn to the first epistle of John, fifth chapter, and read the twentieth verse?" In a sweet voice she read to the eager listeners the verse referring to Christ which says, "This is the true God, and eternal life," being the words which her father said should have been used. The judge gracefully changed the subject, and the discussion was closed.

Mr. McCullagh lived in Monticello, N. Y., several years, where he taught school and worked among the poor in Sullivan and the adjoining counties. The following incident will illustrate the nature of his work there:

One Sunday he walked six miles through

deep snow, with a load of books on his back, to organize a Sunday-school among the "bark-peelers." They were considered to be such wicked people that it was not worth while to try any religious work among them. But before he commenced his address one of the "bark-peelers" jumped up and said, "This young man has already preached the best sermon in this county. To carry such a load as this six miles through the snow is what I call a 'back-load sermon.' That is the kind of sermon I like. Now I came here to break up the meeting; but we are going to have a Sunday-school here if I have to superintend it myself." Then, shaking his brawny fists at some of his companions, he continued, "If any of you fellows disturb this Sunday-school, see what you will get. Now, young preacher, make your speech and I will keep order." A good and useful Sunday-school was the result. In after years he saw the spire of a church pointing heavenward from the spot where he organized this school.

CHAPTER IV.

GOES WEST.

THE state of Illinois was at that time attracting great attention. Many new railroads were being projected, and many settlers moving into the state. Mr. McCullagh resolved to go to Illinois, believing that much greater destitution could be found there than in New York. Owing to the slow methods of transportation then in use, it was a long and tedious journey. Arriving at Pittsburgh, he paid his passage on a steamer to Shawneetown, Illinois.

The boat reached Louisville, Ky., Saturday night. When they were some twenty miles from the city, he went to the captain and said, "How long will you remain at Louisville?"

"I do not know," replied the captain; "why do you ask?"

"Because I have paid my fare to Shawneetown, and if the boat is going on to-night I will get off, as I do not travel on the Sabbath."

The captain looked at him in amazement,

31

and said, "I have been running steamboats for many years, but you are the first man I have met who would get off, after his fare was paid, to keep from travelling on Sunday; but I respect you for it—I had a good mother, if I am a hard sinner. I have a large amount of iron and other freight for parties in Louisville. If they are ready to receive it when we arrive, the boat goes on in a few hours. It will be late when we get there, and if the parties have gone home, we will not leave Louisville until Monday morning. I will let you know."

After the boat landed, the captain came to Mr. McCullagh and said, "We cannot get away from here before Monday. Do not tell the passengers; they will worry me about it."

The first Sunday in Kentucky proved to be a memorable one in Mr. McCullagh's life. He visited the Second Presbyterian Church Sunday-school, and made an address at the close. He heard Rev. Dr. E. P. Humphrey, pastor of the church, preach an able sermon from the text, "For I am not ashamed of the gospel of Christ: for it is the power of God unto salvation to every one that believeth" (Romans 1 : 16).

With this seemingly accidental tarry at Louisville were connected far-reaching results. In
after years this Presbyterian church Sunday-
school became a regular contributor to his work,
and continues it to this day. This school alone
has given thousands of dollars to the American
Sunday-School Union, besides a large amount
regularly contributed by the members of the
church. Dr. Humphrey became Mr. McCullagh's life-long friend, and a regular contributor;
and many years after gave this cordial endorse-
ment of his work: "The American Sunday-
School Union for fifty-nine years has carried the
gospel to thousands who had no other instruction
in the plan of salvation. Its missionary work
has been managed through the South with sin-
gular discretion and ability, and its opportunity
was never so great as now."

About forty years later, Mr. McCullagh
visited the Sunday-school of the College Street
Presbyterian Church, of which Dr. Humphrey
was then the pastor. In closing his address
he said, "I desire to offer a challenge to this
school. Forty years ago I heard your pastor
preach a sermon, and I venture to say I can

3

tell more of that sermon than any of you teachers or scholars can repeat of any sermon the doctor has preached in the last four weeks. Dr. Humphrey is here, and he will be the judge. Any one who is ready will please begin."

He paused, waiting for some one to commence. There was no response.

Dr. Humphrey then came forward, and was deeply affected. He said, "I regard this, Brother McCullagh, as the compliment of my life; that you, a stranger, forty years ago passing through Louisville, having heard me preach, should remember the text and all the points of my sermon." In a private conversation which followed, Mr. McCullagh, in a bantering way, said, "Doctor, I heard you preach recently, and you are preaching about the same old subjects you did years ago. Why don't you preach about the sensations and new things?"

"Ah," said the doctor, "God's love for sinners and the great salvation through Christ will be my theme as long as I live."

Rev. Dr. Stuart Robinson, who was after-

wards pastor of the Second Presbyterian
Church, was also the beloved friend and cordial helper of Mr. McCullagh in his Sunday-
school work. Some years he personally contributed fifty dollars to the cause.

In May, 1875, Dr. Robinson went to New
York city and delivered an address, pleading
for the support of the American Sunday-School
Union in the South. The meeting was held
in the Academy of Music. The vast and
beautiful building was crowded to its utmost
capacity. Hon. William E. Dodge was the
chairman of the evening, and every seat on
the great platform was occupied. Among
those present were Drs. John Hall, Armitage,
Deems, J. Cotton Smith, and also Messrs.
Morris K. Jesup, F. Marquand, Alexander
Brown, Maurice A. Wurts, Edwin W. Rice,
and other officers and managers of the society.

When this noble man passed away, Mr.
McCullagh felt that he had lost a true friend,
a sincere sympathizer, a brother beloved; and
he wept for him as David did for Jonathan.

Other pastors and Sunday-schools in after
days were drawn into cordial sympathy with

the missionary work of the society. The War-
ren Memorial Sunday-school, Preston Street
Union Mission, Walnut Street Presbyterian
school, Park Mission school, and others also became interested in Mr. McCullagh's work, and
were liberal contributors.

On his regular visits he made many friends
in all the churches in Louisville, and among
the business men generally. The sum which
he raised in that city, for the American Sunday-School Union, amounts to more than forty
thousand dollars.

Great results sometimes spring from small
beginnings. By his determination not to travel
on Sunday he became connected with these
noble workers, which led to important results.

CHAPTER V.

IN ILLINOIS.

THE events narrated in the last chapter interrupted the orderly course of our history; but they illustrate the truth of the Scripture, "Them that honour me I will honour, and they that despise me shall be lightly esteemed" (1 Samuel 2 : 30).

Let us resume our narrative. The boat left Louisville on Monday morning, and Mr. McCullagh arrived safely at Shawneetown. He at once entered the corps of civil engineers engaged in constructing a railroad running out from Shawneetown. The country through which they worked was infected with malaria. Chills and bilious fever were almost epidemic. Their fare consisted of bacon and corn-bread. The five engineers with whom he worked were all healthy and robust. After their hard work these men ate heartily of this coarse food, but Mr. McCullagh partook very sparingly of it. In a short time four of them were taken with

the fever and died; the remaining one returned
to the East.   Soon afterwards Mr. McCullagh
had his first chill.   It was amusing to hear him
describe it.   He had never seen any one with
the ague until he lived in Illinois.

He went with Mr. Crenshaw, a good old
Methodist brother, to a camp-meeting which
was then being held.   A camp-meeting was
something entirely new to him; he had never
heard of one in Scotland.   One day at the
meeting, about noon, Mr. McCullagh had a hard
chill.   Mr. Crenshaw said, " Brother Mac, you
know what a chill is now, and they are not very
funny.   Come, I must take you home; you are
in for a hard spell of illness."   This good man
was right; chill followed chill, and resulted in
a violent attack of fever.   He was sick many
weeks, and it was thought he could not recover.
Great suffering was caused from the despond-
ency and depression which malarial poison pro-
duces.

Mr. Crenshaw nursed him like a brother.
During the weary days of his convalescence
Mr. McCullagh said, " Brother Crenshaw, I do
not believe I am going to get well."

"Tut! nonsense, man!" he replied. "God has a great work for you to do. You are not going to die until that work is done." In a strong, sweet voice he would begin to sing:

"Come, my soul, thy suit prepare,
   Jesus loves to answer prayer;
   He himself has bid thee pray,
   Therefore will not say thee nay.

"Thou art coming to a King,
   Large petitions with thee bring;
   For his grace and power are such,
   None can ever ask too much."

Then this good man would get on his knees and, with the tears streaming down his cheeks, pray that God would comfort the spirit and heal the body of the sick brother. As Mr. McCullagh often expressed it, "Brother Crenshaw could sing like a thrush, and out-pray the natives."

The patient improved slowly. Finally, Brother Crenshaw said, "Mac, you have been in that bed long enough. To-morrow morning, at five o'clock, my son Bill will have the horse at the door, and you are to be up and dressed, and he will drive you four miles just after sun-up."

"Why, Brother Crenshaw, I could not get up if you would give me your farm."

"You are in my house, sir, and my word is law."

The next morning, at half-past four o'clock, Brother Crenshaw's commanding tones were heard: "Get up quick, Bill, and go get the horse; Mac will be ready in a few minutes, and you must drive him four miles before breakfast." These words brought despair to the heart of the poor sufferer. He feebly arose and began to dress. In a short time he was going to the gate, leaning on Mr. Crenshaw's arm. When he returned from the drive the sun looked brighter and the birds sang more sweetly than he had ever known. Brother Crenshaw's heroic treatment was just what was needed; and after continuing it some time, the patient improved wonderfully. He never ceased to love this good man for his kindness, and always held him in grateful remembrance.

Mr. McCullagh now commenced his Sunday-school work in southern Illinois in earnest. This region was called "Egypt," on account of the moral darkness which prevailed in that section. He commenced vigorous work in Massac county, where a large number of outlaws had settled. They were called "Flatheads," and had a majority in some of the precincts, and could elect one of their number as county offi- cer. It was regarded unsafe to take a good horse into the county, for it was sure to be claimed by one of the "Flatheads." The case would be tried before an "esquire" or local magistrate and a jury who were "Flatheads." Of course the traveller would lose his horse. Mr. McCullagh, strange to say, was cordially welcomed, and organized a number of Sunday- schools among these people. Some of the grand- est results of his life-work were accomplished in "Egypt."

While laboring in Illinois he made the ac- quaintance of Abraham Lincoln. He heard him deliver political speeches, and on one oc- casion carried him a number of miles in his Sunday-school buggy. When he told Mr. Lin- coln that he intended to move to Kentucky, he replied, "God bless old Kentuck! God bless old Kentuck! it is my native state."

CHAPTER VI.

HAVING heard much about Kentucky, her whole-souled people and her religious destitution, Mr. McCullagh resolved to make that his permanent home. In November, 1839, he moved to Henderson county.

During the winter he organized his first Sunday-school in Kentucky. It was started in a school-house not far from where "Posey Chapel" church now stands. About the time the school was fairly organized for work, a flock of sheep, grazing near by, which had taken possession of the school-room the day before, were chased by some dogs. They, to flee for safety, made a break for the school-house. The door was open and they rushed in, the old ram leading them; but finding it occupied, he ran on through the house and jumped out of the window, and the whole flock followed him.

In March, 1840, Mr. McCullagh moved to the town of Henderson, which continued to be

42

his home through life. At this time there was no Sunday-school in Henderson, and none in Kentucky for a distance of seventy-five miles, except the little one that he had started in the county. The destitution stirred his soul. He soon announced that a Sunday-school meeting would be held in the old seminary. On Sunday, an hour before the meeting, he went up and down the streets with a hand-bell, like an auctioneer, urging the people to come. This Union school, which he organized, superintended and fostered, had a remarkable history. It proved to be a marvellous power for good. It continued as a Union school for a number of years. As the town grew and the various denominations increased in strength, they gradually withdrew to organize schools of their own. This old Union school was the forerunner of the ten churches and fourteen Sunday-schools now in Henderson. Many of the office-bearers and prominent members in these churches studied their first Bible lesson in the old Union school.

In the spring of 1840 Mr. McCullagh opened the Henderson Eclectic Institute, a school for

young men and boys. The success of this enterprise was phenomenal. Good teachers were
scarce in those times. His school was soon
filled with the most promising young men of
Henderson and the surrounding country, and it
became necessary for him to engage assistants.
He continued this school, which was a growing
success, until he gave it up to devote his whole
time to the work of The American Sunday-
School Union. The influence for good which
he exerted in the school-room cannot be estimated. Starling's History of Henderson says:
"A majority of the young men of the town, at
that time, owe their education to Rev. John
McCullagh. He worked indefatigably in the
interest of educating the young. He was ex-
tremely popular with the children, and was perhaps the best-known man in the county. He
took great pride in his scholars, and affectionately spoke of them as 'my boys.' Many of
them have held high positions of honor and
trust; some being ministers, congressmen, law-
yers, bankers and merchants."

His Sunday-school work during this time was
simply amazing. Western Kentucky was de-

veloping rapidly, and many new settlers were moving in. He was constantly pushing forward vigorously to start a Sunday-school at every new point. On Friday afternoon his pony " Charry" was hitched to the fence. As soon as school closed he was off to an adjoining county, and would ride probably thirty miles that afternoon and evening. On Saturday he would be riding in every direction, visiting the people, making Sunday-school speeches at country stores and spreading the notice of his appointments. On Sunday he would organize probably two schools six or eight miles apart, and start for home late in the afternoon, sometimes not getting back before midnight. Monday morning, with a smiling face, he would be ready to open school.

The hardships in this work were often very great. Sometimes when in the midst of the forest, ten o'clock at night, miles from any house, a great storm would break upon him, the darkness black as Egypt and the rain falling in torrents; his pony would tremble like a leaf at the mighty bursts of thunder and the falling of the trees around them. The missionary would often be forced to stop for an hour, drenched with the rain, waiting for the fury of the tempest to subside, so as to make it safe to proceed.

Another difficulty was to keep in the right way. The country was new, covered with forests, and the roads very poor and circuitous. Some one has aptly said, "The roads in these parts for the first mile or two were pretty good, for the next three miles they were rough, and then they dwindled down to a bridle-path; after that they were not much more than a sheep-track; then they faded into a squirrel-track, and at last they ran up a tree." A witty man once told him, "This road commences here and ends 'nowhar.'"

On one occasion, having lost his way, he saw a cabin in the midst of a corn-field. He shouted "Halloo!" but no one heard him. He then dismounted and, getting over the fence, started for the house. When about half way, two fierce dogs rushed toward him. What could he do? To run meant to be torn in pieces, to stand still seemed to be the same. There was a fallen tree lying near. He jumped behind the tree, and took off his straw hat and waved it rapidly at the enraged dogs. For a moment they seemed to fear there was some hidden evil in the hat, but their courage soon revived. When he struck one dog in the face with the hat to make him stay on his own side of the log, he tore a piece out of it. By this time the other dog was nearly over and required the attention of the hat, from which he also took a piece. The hat was being rapidly torn into shreds. To his great joy he was soon reinforced by a man, who came running from the cabin, with a big club, and beat the dogs into subjection, and gave the missionary full directions, so that he went on his way rejoicing.

FIRST PRESBYTERIAN CHURCH, HENDERSON, KY.

PRIMITIVE SCHOOL-HOUSE IN KENTUCKY.

CHAPTER VII.

As it was with the apostles, who commenced their work in Jerusalem, so Mr. McCullagh regarded his own home as the proper place to begin Christian effort. After getting the Henderson Union Sunday-school into successful operation, his next step was to build a church. The facts connected with this effort are taken from the excellent article in "Starling's History of Henderson," prepared by W. J. Marshall.

In 1840 there were about fifteen or twenty Presbyterians scattered through Henderson county. The Posey brothers and their families, and a few mothers in Israel, still clung to the covenant.

"At this time," says the above history, "a young stranger, whom, it seems, a kind Providence had especially fitted and sent to accomplish a great work for the Church, came to Henderson. He made friends wherever he went, and ere long he had gained both the

4   49

esteem and confidence of the whole community. I allude to John McCullagh, to whom, under God, the Church at Henderson owes more, for the prosperity she has since enjoyed, than to any other person. Being an earnest worker, he could not sit by contented while the cause of Zion languished, her people being as sheep without a shepherd, having no spiritual home.

"The Sunday-school which he had organized was a success, and the enthusiasm of this young brother was contagious, and soon manifested itself in the church. His motto was, 'Expect great things from God; attempt great things for God.' He had a church meeting held, at which new officers were elected, and arrangements were made with Rev. J. V. Dodge to preach for them.

"Mr. McCullagh's next move was to build a church, that was not to cost less than six thousand dollars; he agreeing to raise money. It was a bold move. It was moreover regarded by many as absurd and preposterous, for a church organization, with a handful of scattered members, to talk about building a six thousand dollar church in a sleepy village.

That amount of money, in those times and circumstances, was as large a sum as fifty thousand dollars would be at the present time. It was a bold enterprise; but in its boldness lay its strength. The church members gave nobly, and the community, pleased at the prospect of such a substantial improvement, responded with liberal subscriptions.

"To raise the money, however, was no easy undertaking; and he resolved to hazard it all on one bold move, which, if accomplished, would give the assurance of success. He got up a paper on which he was to have two thousand dollars subscribed by not more than ten persons; the subscriptions were not to be binding unless the whole amount was raised within sixty days.

"After gleaning the field, he had seventeen hundred dollars subscribed by nine persons. He was now in a dilemma, and knew not where to go. He speaks of it as follows: 'In this dark and trying hour I went to the mercy-seat for light, and spent a sleepless night wrestling in prayer. In the early dawn the light came. A voice seemed to say, "Go

and see Mrs. R. B. Stites, and tell her your
desire to secure 'a place for the Lord, an hab-
itation for the mighty God of Jacob.' It all
depends upon her; she will not refuse." I
went without delay, and was cordially received.
She inquired how I was getting on in raising the
two thousand dollars. With a sad heart and
in trembling words I attempted to tell her the
exact state of the case; that, so far as I knew,
everything depended on some *one* of God's
jewels giving the balance of the two thousand
dollars. I talked on and on, at great length,
fearing to give her a chance to refuse. She
seemed greatly amused, and at last replied,
"Well, my young brother, I knew what you
came for, and what all this long talk meant.
You shall have the three hundred dollars, with
great pleasure. I laid it aside for you, and
now just go ahead and raise the four thousand
dollars." (I started off singing the long-metre
doxology, shouting now and then, "Glory,
Hallelujah!"')

"He raised the money. The church was
built; and when it was dedicated a glorious
revival followed, and some fifty of the most

prominent citizens were converted. This church has continued to grow and prosper, until it is now among the strongest churches in Kentucky."

In 1884, the congregation having outgrown their church building, a colony went out to organize the Second Presbyterian Church. Mr. McCullagh was in cordial sympathy with the plan, and aided it both by contributions and by wise counsel. This church now has over two hundred members, and owns property worth twelve thousand dollars.

For more than forty years he visited annually every Sunday-school or church in the town, or would hold mass meetings to which all were invited. These meetings were largely attended. In his earnest, thrilling manner he recounted the progress and triumph of the Sunday-school cause during the year. As he poured out a tide of facts, which he called "God's arguments," there were few who did not receive fresh inspiration, and make new resolutions to enlarge their Christian effort in the future.

In March, 1852, a writer for the *Sunday-*

School Journal, then published by the American Sunday-School Union, in describing one of these Union meetings, after giving an account of Mr. McCullagh's address, says, "The rector of the Episcopal church arose and said, 'I call upon all to hold up the hands of the Sunday-school missionary, as Aaron and Hur held up the hands of Moses. I will stand on one side of Brother McCullagh; who will stand on the other? I will hold up one of his hands; who will hold up the other?' The Presbyterian minister said, 'The time for making speeches in behalf of the American Sunday-School Union has gone by; its great utility is acknowledged by all.' He urged the audience to contribute liberally to the cause. The Baptist minister said, 'That as long as this great work was well sustained there was no danger in the future for our country.' The Cumberland Presbyterian minister expressed his hearty co-operation in this work. The pastor of the Methodist church made an address full of timely suggestions."

There are but few persons who have been raised in Henderson county who did not know

Mr. McCullagh, and cannot recall his Sunday-school stories.

Shortly after coming to Henderson, he met Miss Lucy M. Lyne, a handsome young lady. He fell in love with her at first sight, but for conscience's sake held his affections in check. (At that time she was fond of attending balls and theatres; and he felt that a woman of the world could not sympathize with his work, nor be a proper help meet in such a cause.) He still loved her secretly. About a year after this, one morning at breakfast, some one asked him if he had heard the news. "No," he replied; "what is it?"

"Why, Miss Lucy Lyne has joined the church, and has given up worldly amusements."

He restrained all feelings of joy, but resolved to press his suit. In this he was successful; and they were married, February 16, 1842. She was a devoted wife, and entered heartily into the spirit of his Sunday-school work. Six children were born to them, three of whom have entered into rest. His absence from home on long missionary trips greatly increased her responsibilities in the care of the large family of little children. She knew how greatly his life was endangered by the accidents of travel and the hardships which he encountered, and was fully aware of her own unprotected condition when he was away. But she was a woman of great moral courage, of sober judgment, of an earnest spiritual nature and fervent piety. She lived a beautiful life of faith and consecration. She died February, 1859. Her last words were, " Precious Jesus, all is well."

His love for her amounted almost to idolatry, and he never married again. One night, about twenty-eight years after her death, he was telling of some of the dangers he had encountered, and of some remarkable escapes he had made. He said, " I cannot understand it; these things seem almost incredible." Just then he looked up at her portrait, hanging over the mantel, and said, with tears in his eyes, " Oh yes, it is she. 'Are they not all ministering spirits sent forth to minister for them who shall be heirs of salvation?' She has been my blessed guardian angel." He then quoted these beautiful lines :

Alone I walk the peopled city,
  Where each seems happy with his own;
O friends, I ask not for your pity,—
    I walk alone.

The gold is rifled from the coffer,
  The blade is stolen from the sheath;
Life has but one more boon to offer,
    And that is death.

Yet well I know the voice of duty,
  And therefore life and health must crave,
Though she who gave the world its beauty
    Is in her grave.

I live, O lost one, for the living
  Who drew their earliest life from thee;
And wait until with glad thanksgiving
    I shall be free.

For life to me is but a station,
  Wherein apart a traveller stands,
One absent long from home and nation—
    In other lands,

And I, as he who stands and listens,
  Amid the twilight's chill and gloom,
To hear, approaching in the distance,
    The train for home.

For death shall bring another meeting,
  Beyond the shadows of the tomb;
On yonder shore is she now waiting,
    Until I come.

CHAPTER VIII.

DURING all the years in which young McCullagh had been working as a volunteer missionary, he bought large supplies of books from the American Sunday-School Union. After coming to Kentucky, his purchases had increased largely until 1841, when they attracted the attention of Rev. J. H. Huber, of Louisville, Ky., superintendent of the society's work in the South.

Mr. Huber came to Henderson, as he expressed it, "to find out something about the young man who was ordering so many Union books and papers for Sunday-schools in and around Henderson." He inquired, "Who gave you authority to organize Union Sabbath-schools?" Mr. McCullagh replied, "I hold my commission from the great Shepherd himself, and it reads as follows, 'Feed my lambs.' I claim only to be a volunteer."

Mr. Huber promptly replied, "I came to

Henderson for no other purpose than to get you to enlist in the *regular army* of the American Sunday-School Union, and I do not intend to leave town until the object of my visit has been accomplished. A man who loves the work so much as to labor for years without a cent of pay cannot fail to make a good permanent missionary."

After considering the many advantages which would result from working as an authorized agent of the society, Mr. McCullagh accepted a commission to labor in Kentucky, at a salary of one dollar per day for each day that he worked. He often said, "I then enlisted not for one year, nor for three years, nor for thirty years, but for life. And I want my name to remain on the roll of the army of the American Sunday-School Union, like the Huguenot captain who received his death-wound on the battle-field. His last request to his superior officer was that his name should remain on the roll of the regiment, and when he was called his comrade should step out of the ranks and say, 'Here—died on the battle-field.'"*

* Mr. McCullagh's son, the Rev. Joseph H. McCullagh,

Great as had been his efforts before, he now felt that they must be redoubled. If, as a volunteer, he had been like Saul, and slain thousands of the enemies of righteousness; as a commissioned missionary, he must be like David, and slay his tens of thousands. His missionary trips became longer and more extended, reaching remote and destitute points. In 1846, the Sunday-school Missionary Association of the Second Presbyterian Church, Louisville, an auxiliary in the work of The American Sunday-School Union, pledged to pay him three hundred dollars for two hundred days' work, he bearing his own travelling expenses. As the result of these two hundred days' labor, he organized fifty new Sunday-schools, containing three thousand one hundred and seventy-four teachers and scholars.

These schools were distributed in eight counties of Kentucky, three of Indiana, and one of Illinois. In one year he organized ninety new schools, with a membership of six thousand

now answers to the roll-call of his father's name, and stands in his father's place as his faithful successor in the society's southern work.—EDITOR.

nine hundred and twenty-six persons. During his labors he organized schools in seventy-five counties in Kentucky, and also many schools through southern Indiana and Illinois.

Nearly all the travel required to accomplish this work was done on horseback, and great hardships were endured. In speaking of it, he says, "I have often gone three months with one suit of clothes; saddle-bags packed with shirts, collars, etc., and a few books, my main supply being sent ahead: so that on getting soaking wet, which was not an unusual occurrence, I had to let my clothes dry on my back. I swam rivers and creeks, at the risk of my life, to reach an appointment."

The years from 1841 to 1852, during which time he thus worked as a missionary for the society, are in some respects the most interesting portion of his life. In the chapters that are to follow, we will endeavor to glean a few sheaves from this great harvest-field of facts and adventure. It is sufficient now to say, in a general way, that his reputation as a Sunday-school preacher soon spread over Kentucky. Whenever he made an appointment, even though it was at a place he had never visited, there was sure to be a crowd. Those who opposed the work would come because they had heard that he was a "mighty interesting speaker, and was a great man for facts." Men, women and children came, some mothers bringing their babies. At one time he counted twenty babies lying asleep about the platform where he was speaking.

His social intercourse with the people was as effective as his public addresses. He was received with great hospitality. After arriving at the house of his host, it was not long before he asked for the good book, to conduct family worship. He soon made friends with all the children, and learned their names, and delighted them with interesting stories. When it was known that he was to stop at a certain house, a number of the neighbors would find it convenient to make a short call of several hours, "just to hear that man talk." During the long summer afternoons or far into the night, his little audience, with the colored people standing at the door, listened with deep interest to his anecdotes. Nor were these mere talks, but, in fact, household sermons disguised to suit the capacity of his audiences. Many a spiritual truth was fixed in their memory with a thrilling fact. Sunday-schools, temperance, history and religion were the web and woof of his theme. In an adroit way, he dealt the prevailing vices of the community deadly strokes, and cheered and aroused God's people.

CHAPTER IX.

On one occasion he made an appointment to organize a Sunday-school at a district school-house in Union county. When he arrived, several hundred people were assembled in the yard. The windows were all nailed down hard and fast, and the door nailed up with heavy boards and spikes. Three big, rough-looking men came up and said, "Are you the Sunday-school man?"

"Yes, I am."

"Well, we wish to ask you one question: do you propose to teach the Bible in your school?"

"Most assuredly I do. Who ever heard of a Sunday-school without the Bible? Where did you fellows come from? The Bible is to be our text-book."

"Well," they replied, "that is what the priest told us. He said you wanted the people to study that wicked book. We are Catholics,

64

and we three are the trustees of this school, and we have nailed up the doors, and you shall never carry the Bible into that house."

Mr. McCullagh was thoroughly indignant, and mounting a stump cried out, "Friends and fellow citizens,—ye who believe the Bible to be the word of God and the only hope of our republic,—hearken unto me. We are law-abiding citizens; let us leave the school grounds and adjourn to yon grove."

The whole crowd followed him—the Catholics also going from curiosity. He there delivered a magnetic and earnest address upon the history and aims of the Romish Church, illustrating its cruelty, bigotry and superstition. These points were all riveted with telling facts, which he had witnessed in Ireland and elsewhere. (He showed that the tendency of Popery was to drag its people down to poverty and ignorance.) Some of the Catholics attempted to interrupt him; but so keen were his retorts that they soon kept still.

To illustrate one of his points he said, "They have a legend in Europe that a man went to sleep in the days of the Reformation, and that

5

he slept for more than two hundred years. He awoke a short time ago and commenced visiting different countries. He went to Protestant England and Scotland and Prussia. The changes were so great that he believed he had waked up on another planet. Railroads, telegraphs, steamboats, trade and commerce, schools, colleges and manufactories were found on every side. 'This cannot be the same world,' he said. He then went to Spain and Italy. 'Yes, indeed, I am in the same world. This is old Spain, just as I left her two hundred years ago: no enterprise; everything dead; eighty per cent. of the people can neither read nor write. The same old Romish Church still has full sway. This is old Italy, where the pope has been ruler for a thousand years. Seventy-three per cent. of the people cannot read; and this glorious land is swarming with beggars.' Ah, my friends, what is it that makes the difference in these countries?"

"It is the Bible," the crowd shouted.

"Yet," cried he, "this same old man of the Tiber is at work in this country. Look at that school-house door nailed up to keep out the

Bible. By the grace of God, and with the help of intelligent American citizens, I purpose to organize a Sunday-school in this grove to-day that shall act as a *claw-hammer* to draw out those nails of ignorance and superstition."

The school was started, and at the election which was held shortly after, the three Catholic trustees were defeated and three Protestant trustees elected. This "claw-hammer" Sunday-school pulled out the nails, and the Bible went into the school-house.

The circulation of religious books he regarded as one of the most important features of the work. He was accustomed to say, "Who can estimate the power and influence of a good book? When the living minister delivers a gospel sermon to a few hundred people, he uses the means ordained of God for their conversion. Then let him commit the thoughts and arguments which God has blessed, to the printer, and by their multiplication through the press he becomes the preacher of a thousand sermons. On the day of Pentecost three thousand were converted by Peter's spoken sermon; but who shall tell us of the tens of thousands who have been blessed by reading the printed report of that remarkable discourse ?"

It was McCullagh's object to induce his Sunday-schools to purchase good books to the extent of their ability. These he supplemented by donations from the society. He also scattered books and papers by the wayside and in the homes he visited. The following will illustrate what some of these books accomplished:

The Books in the Furrow.—When riding along Highland Creek, he suddenly came to a clearing, and saw a man plowing in the field. The man was cursing his mules at a terrible rate. Mr. McCullagh perceived he was half drunk, and looking in his saddle-bags found two books published by the society—"The Drama of Drunkenness" and "Ralph Moore, the Profane Boy." The plowman soon went around the hill with his team. McCullagh dismounted and ran to the furrow in which the plow should come in the round. He opened the books, placed them in the furrow, and then ran hastily back and concealed himself behind a tree to see what would happen.

When the mules came near the books they stopped and snorted and jumped to one side. The man again swore at them, but soon went around to see what had frightened them.

"Two books!" said he with a rough exclamation. "How did they get here?" He looked around in every direction, but could see no one; then stood gazing up into the sky to see if they had dropped down from there. Finally he sat down on the beam of his plow to look at the pictures, and commenced to read the books. The missionary withdrew unperceived, wondering what would be the result of this arrow from a bow drawn at a venture.

About a year after this occurrence he organized a Sunday-school within three miles of this place. When the library was opened, a man came forward and looking into one of the books saw the name of the American Sunday-School Union, and asked, "Mr. McCullagh, did you pass along Highland Creek about a year ago? If so, you must go home with me; I have something to show you."

On reaching the house he brought out the two books, saying, "Did you ever see these before?"

He replied, " Yes."

"Well, sir," said Uncle Ben, "I have lost a heap by reading them."

Mr. McCullagh inquired, "What did you lose ?"

He replied, " On reading these two books, I took an oath on my knees in that furrow, that I would never taste a drop of liquor while I lived. I then had a very bad name, a very red face, a bad habit of swearing, an aching head, a heavy heart, a guilty conscience, and a drunkard's home. Now I have lost every one of them. I have gained something too, thank God. I now have a good name and a happy home; but better than all, my wife, our two daughters and myself have all found the Pearl of great price. It was that verse in the story of Ralph Moore, 'The blood of Jesus Christ . . . cleanseth us from all sin,' which brought us all to the cross."

Uncle Ben became an active member of the church and the superintendent of two Sabbath-schools.

CHAPTER X.

The Travellers' Rest.—On one of his missionary trips, he visited Richmond, Ky., and held a Sunday-school meeting, in which he told them of his work in the mountains. At the close, a collection was taken up, and only fifteen dollars was received.

The pastor of the Presbyterian church arose and said, "Ten times this amount should be given to this cause. I am going to give this brother ten dollars myself to help start a Sunday-school in Clay county. Last year I was directed by the presbytery to go there and preach. The appointment was duly made, and after a long and fatiguing ride I reached it, and found that I had an audience of three persons, two ladies and one child. On inquiring where all the men and boys spent their Sabbaths, I was informed that they were at a tavern called 'The Travellers' Rest,' where they were drinking and engaging in various sports. I could do

71

nothing there. I desire this brother to try the Sunday-school method of reform in that place."

Mr. McCullagh started for this hard field, and went straight to The Travellers' Rest and had his horse put up. The landlord said, " So, you are the preacher; going to preach here next Sunday?"

"Yes, and organize a Sunday-school," Mr. McCullagh replied.

"All right," said the landlord; "I will see that you have a big crowd. You are not one of those stuck-up fellows that come around occasionally. I will send out all my chaps and drum you up a crowd."

On Sunday the house was filled, and McCullagh made his address. Toward the close he said, "I understand that you already have a Sunday-school in this place; but it is the wrong kind. The men and boys attend school at 'The Travellers' Rest,' and there they learn to drink, gamble, swear and fight.

"The kind of Sunday-school that I propose to start graduates its scholars as upright Christian men into the Church of God. 'The Travellers' Rest' sends out its graduates also. A short time ago, two young men, convicted for murder, were sent to the penitentiary for seven years. This murder was committed at 'The Travellers' Rest,' and the man who sold them liquor is guilty as a partaker in the crime; he is in this house to-day."

The mothers of these two boys were sitting just in front of him, and were sobbing aloud. The landlord of "The Travellers' Rest" was but a few steps from him. Mr. McCullagh turned suddenly toward him and said, "You are the man who has robbed these mothers of their sons. You are the man who is carrying on this carnival of vice and crime, desecrating God's holy day, and making criminals of the men and boys of this place. These are your graduates; some are now in the state prison. Look at your work!"

Then a man suddenly cried out, "Move him." And the cry became general, "Move him." Mr. McCullagh was puzzled to know which one they intended to move, the landlord or himself. The landlord, however, was not in doubt; so he seized his hat and rushed out. Many followed him, and warned him to make his arrangements to leave the place or he would be severely dealt with. He accordingly left.

Mr. McCullagh, continuing his address, said, "I have learned things about the sad case of these two boys in prison, which, if they were known by the governor of the state, I believe would lead him to pardon them. If you will get up a petition stating these mitigating circumstances, I will go to Frankfort before long and will present it to Governor Powell, who is my friend and neighbor, and I hope we may be able to restore those boys to their homes. We will start our Sunday-school by trying to undo the sad work of 'The Travellers' Rest.'"

A good school was organized, and a few months afterward the governor pardoned the two boys.

Filling Appointments.—During forty years' work he failed but once to fill an appointment. This was as late as 1883, when he started in good time for Wheeling, West Va. He spent the Sabbath in Louisville, and addressed several schools. That evening he was taken dangerously ill. The physician advised him to return home as soon as possible, which he did; and for three days and nights his family thought he would cross over the river of death, and rest under the trees. He was very sick for several months.

In speaking of filling appointments, he says, " The importance of punctuality cannot be overrated. Allow me to give an illustration:

"*White Lick School.*—On a bright, sunny Sabbath, many years ago, I organized a Sabbath-school at the Richland meeting-house, in southern Kentucky. I had an appointment for another meeting that afternoon at three o'clock, at White Lick, about fifteen miles from Richland. Although I received sundry pressing invitations in accordance with the old-fashioned *genuine* hospitality so *universal* in Kentucky, 'Come home and stay with us,' yet I declined, fearing that I might not reach the Lick in time; and snatching a hasty snack from my saddle-bags, started for the timber, our good brother E., an old Sunday-school worker, having kindly offered to guide the missionary through the trackless woods. So away we went at the double-quick, in single file, over logs, through brush and swamps swarming with reptiles.

" Suddenly the air began to darken ; a curious cloud was seen in the west. My guide exclaimed, 'I do believe a tornado is coming *this way*, and if we are caught in the timber we may be crushed to death. We must *ride for life.*' Our horses seemed to know that danger was near, and dashed ahead at a fearful rate, but we were soon compelled to stop and take shelter in a rough cabin, erected by hunters a few months before. Yes, there it comes with deafening peals of thunder. How grand! how fearful! how terrific! how it sweeps and levels the forest! The giant oak of a century is torn and twisted as if it were a sapling.

> ' He plants his footsteps in the sea,
> And rides upon the storm.'

But the cabin under the cliff was a safe hiding-place for us. ' Well, we have been miraculously protected,' said the brother, 'and so will every poor sinner be secure who takes refuge under the shadow of the " Rock of Ages." '

" After getting through the fallen timber, my good friend remarked, 'Well now, let us take the back track for it.' 'What is that for ?' I

inquired. 'Because we can't get to the Lick
before six o'clock, and the congregation won't
wait three hours for us, I know.' 'Well,
Brother E., that may be all true, but I'm going
on there anyhow.' Forward, march! and away
we went at a gallop. What a grand sight we
saw on our arrival! We found a crowd still
waiting and *watching* for the preacher. We had
a very precious meeting, and organized a Sabbath-school. After the benediction, my guide
inquired of the superintendent, 'How on earth
did you all come to wait so long for us?'
'Well, brother,' he replied, 'I was at M.'s last
week, and inquired of friend W. if he thought
the Sunday-school man would come all the way
down to the Lick. "Yes," said brother W.;
"don't be uneasy about that; the old war-horse
will be there, even if he has to swim Trade-
water." We saw the storm passing round toward Richland, and some of the *sugar* and *salt*
ones suggested we had better go home; but on
hearing what *Wilkins* said of the old chap's
punctuality, they determined to wait on even
until dark.' *A large working church was the
result of filling that appointment.*"

CHAPTER XI.

INCIDENTS OF THE WORK.

A COMMON difficulty in this mission work was to find suitable officers for the schools when they were organized. When the right man was found, Mr. McCullagh would take no excuse. The following will illustrate his persistence:

Bright Light.—While organizing the "Bright Light" Sunday-school in Union county, he was describing the duties and qualifications of the person whom they should elect superintendent. Before the vote was taken, an elderly gentleman arose and said:

"Whoever you elect superintendent may just as well accept at once, for the old missionary will never let him off. He came to my place twenty-nine years ago and asked me to superintend a Sunday-school at the coal mines. I told him, 'No, I could not do it;' but he talked on and on. Whenever I got a chance to put in a word, I said, 'No; I can't.' But he kept on talking until after midnight.

78

"When I showed him up to his room, I said to myself, 'Well, young man, I am safe now; for I will be off to Morganfield before you are up.' But, lo and behold, I found him cutting wood early in the morning. I told him I was on the grand jury, and had to be in Morganfield by ten o'clock. He replied, 'Very well, I will ride part of the way with you.'

"After starting, he commenced his old talk, and I continued to say, 'No; I can't.' On reaching the big flat, which was a mile wide and covered with water nearly deep enough to swim a horse, I said, 'This will stop him sure;' but he plunged right in and followed me to the other side. When we reached dry land, I said, 'I see that you are in blood earnest, and I will have to do the best I can for that school.' He grasped my hand in both of his, and exclaimed, 'May God bless you, Brother Johnston! I must now go to Caseyville, where I have an appointment for to-night. This is twenty miles out of my way, but I would have followed you for a hundred miles, until I had your consent to superintend that school.' I tell you, my friends, there is no dodging that brother."

The moment he sat down, a gentleman moved that Esquire Johnston be elected superintendent of the "Bright Light" Sunday-school, which was carried by acclamation. He arose and said, "Well, the old missionary has flanked me again, and I may just as well surrender."

Archie and the Testament.—Mr. McCullagh organized a Sunday-school on Buckhorn Creek, in one of our mountain counties. The next day, when riding about three miles from there, he saw a ragged boy, about twelve years of age, chopping wood by the road-side.

The pony stopped at the sight of the child, and the following interview took place:

"Where do you live?"

"Half a mile up the road, stranger."

"What is your name?"

"My name is Archie."

"Have you any sisters or brothers?"

"Yes, sir; I have three sisters and two brothers. I had a little brother Bennie, but he died not long ago; and they dug a deep hole and put poor little brother down in that dark place."

"Have you a day-school here?"

" No, sir."

" Any Sunday-school ?"

" No, sir."

" Would you like to have a book that tells about a happy world up yonder, where people will never die any more ?"

" That I would, sir."

" Well, here it is," said the missionary, pulling out a little Testament. " Sit down, Archie, and let me tell you about it."

They sat down on the log, and the mountain-boy drank in every word Mr. McCullagh told him of Christ, heaven and eternal life. The little fellow's heart was touched, and looking up, he said, " What is your name, Mr. stranger ?"

On being told, he said, " I have heard tell of you before. You is the man what makes Sunday-schools, ain't you ? I wish I knowed how to read this little book what tells about Jesus."

" Well, my little man, if you will attend the Sunday-school near the bridge, on Buckhorn Creek, they will teach you."

" When do it meet ?" he inquired.

6

"Every Sunday morning at nine o'clock."

"Well, I'll be thar, if I am alive; and I will keep this little book just as long as I live."

After a few more kind words, the missionary rode away.

The next Sabbath, Archie started in search of the Sunday-school. After some time, he met a man who was hunting squirrels, and asked him,

"Have you seen anything of a Sunday-school this way?"

"A what? I don't know what you mean."

"Well, I don't know exactly what it is myself; but it is up near the bridge."

"Oh, it is in the old school-house, I reckon. I saw people going in there."

Archie hurried on, and met the superintendent at the door.

"I want to learn how to read this book," said he, bringing out the Testament.

"All right; walk in."

After two years, Mr. McCullagh visited this place, and found that Archie, his father, mother, three sisters and two brothers were in the Sunday-school, and also his neighbor Bentley and his family.

Mr. B. gave an account of Archie's first interview, and their conversation in the woods, when he was hunting the Sunday-school.

It was eight years before Mr. McCullagh again saw Archie. In the meantime the civil war was raging. One Sabbath afternoon he visited a hospital in one of our cities. In looking down along a long row of cots, he saw the stump of an arm beckoning him. As he drew near, the handsome face of a young man, chastened by suffering, greeted him. "I am Archie, Mr. McCullagh. I have had both of my arms shot off, and they tell me that owing to exposure, neglect and loss of blood, I cannot get well; but it will only be going home to die no more. How sweet are those words in that little Testament, 'I am the resurrection, and the life: he that believeth in me, though he were dead, yet shall he live: and whosoever liveth and believeth in me shall never die!'"

Lost in the Forest.—While travelling in one of our thinly-settled counties, McCullagh lost his way. Night was fast coming on, and he was in the midst of a vast forest. He resolved to cry for help, and shouted "Lost!" as loud as he could. The sound rolled through the forest and died away in the distance; but he continued to shout "Lost!" He heard a voice in the distance say "Lost!" "It is only an echo mocking me," he thought. He listened and heard the voice again crying "Lost!" "It is some one in the same condition that I am."

The two continued to shout and to draw nearer. Soon a man on horseback came in sight. Mr. McCullagh inquired, "Who are you?"

"Oh, praise the Lord! I am a Methodist preacher," was the response. "Who are you?"

"Oh, praise the Lord! I am a Sunday-school missionary, and a heap bigger man than you."

This was responded to by a hearty laugh. They soon entered into serious conversation. It was decided that it would be dangerous to wander through the forest any longer that night, and they must camp out.

"We Methodists always carry the fire with us," said the preacher, bringing out a piece of flint; but after searching in vain, he declared that he had lost his steel.

"Oh, if that is all you want," said Mr.

McCullagh, "here it is," handing him his knife. "In union there is strength : what one lacks the other supplies. Here is a Presbyterian knife to knock the fire out of a Methodist flint."

A good fire was soon started, and the forest resounded with songs of praise. They whiled away the hours by genial conversation, in which Mr. McCullagh reminded his fellow, "You and I, brother, are but scouts, starting the watch-fires of the Redeemer's kingdom in dark places. We are all soldiers in the same army. The day is coming when Satan's kingdom shall fall, and it can only go down under the grand charge of God's united people, Jesus himself leading the solid phalanx."

"Bless the Lord ! that is so," said the Methdist, and commenced singing "Blest be the tie that binds."

CHAPTER XII.

FROM THE MISSIONARY'S NOTE-BOOK.

THERE were few obstacles that deterred McCullagh in the prosecution of his work. He had an appointment at C—— to organize a school. Meeting with a friend who was familiar with the place, he was advised not to attempt it, as there was a distillery near by, and nothing good could be accomplished. Mr. McCullagh replied, "You are entirely wrong. Within the past week I saw a large meeting-house, the result of a Sunday-school which I organized in a dram-shop, in a town where there had not been a sermon preached in three years. I am not afraid to make an effort near a distillery, nor in one; and when it is in full blast too, if an opportunity offered."

He asked his friend to accompany him to the neighborhood. They found a crowd awaiting them, and his friend was greatly astonished to find the owner of the distillery present and voting to have the Sunday-school.

86

Alphabetarians.—In organizing a school in a very destitute locality, he said, " The children were growing up ignorant and vicious, irreligious and profane. I visited every family in the neighborhood, and showed them the importance of having a Sunday-school and a good library. 'What good can books do us?' they replied; 'we cannot read.' I told them to learn to read. 'Not old folks,' said they. I said, 'Yes; I recently organized a Sunday-school, where I entered twelve alphabetarians whose aggregate ages amounted to five hundred and eighty years.' 'We are too poor to buy books, but you come next Sunday and make us a *sarmon* on these things.'

"I found that two leading men were opposed to the effort. I understood they said that I only wanted to make a little money out of them, and that all so-called benevolent societies were just money-making machines.

"During my address on the Sabbath I noticed several weeping. I told them I knew they were not able to buy suitable books, but if they would all promise to come regularly, I would present them with a good library from a friend in New York. The opposers looked at each other in astonishment. 'Will you accept the books on these terms?' 'Yes, and with ten thousand thanks; and may God bless our New York friend.'"

Rough Fare.—A missionary who travels almost constantly in rural districts soon becomes a good judge in selecting suitable stopping-places for meals and lodging; but sometimes the keenest eye is deceived.

In going on a long trip in a new district, Mr. McCullagh stopped at a nice-looking farm-house to see if he could get dinner. The lady said, "Our dinner is over, but I reckon I can get you something." The meal was soon ready, and consisted of cold boiled cabbage, sour buttermilk and corn bread. After eating, he said, "Madam, I wish to pay for my dinner; how much is it?"

"You don't mean to pay for it?" she said.

"Certainly; I am always ready to pay for what I get."

"Why did you not tell me you meant to pay for your dinner?" she exclaimed. "If you had said so, you could have had chicken, and pie, and coffee too."

Uncle Billy and Parson Benton.—At one Sunday-school appointment, Parson Benton had previously given notice that he would attend and expose the whole scheme, and prove it to be a British *consarn* "from a to izzard." Sure enough, the parson spoke in opposition to the Sunday-school. He asserted most positively that Mr. McCullagh was a Britisher from Scotland; Queen Victoria had *sartinly* sent him over to establish these schools all over the country, and in that way her majesty would have a strong claim on old Kentuck. "Keep out of this trap," he exclaimed. "And as for the book larnin', it is wuss than useless. Who can preach longer than your humble sarvant? and he never was in school but six days in his whole life. It costs too much to buy these purty books; we is all too poor; times is too hard and money sca'ce."

At the close of the parson's remarks, an old gentleman, called Uncle Billy, addressed him as follows:

"Brother Benton, did you not hear Mr. McCullagh say a kind friend in the East had paid for these books, and would give us this library?   Now don't that show there must be some good in the Sunday-school work?

"Now, friends, look here and listen to Uncle Billy.   Which is the best friend to us—Mr. Benton, who sells our children and servants whisky by the dram on Sunday, although he says money is so scarce and we are so poor, or Mr. M., in the East, who offers us these beautiful books for nothing?   Every one of them, it seems, teaches us how to make our way home to heaven when we die.   *Who is our best friend?*" shouted Uncle Billy in tones of thunder.

"Mr. M.!" "Mr. M.!" resounded from all parts of the house.

Parson Benton walked out, and Uncle Billy said, "If he does not come back until he is asked, he will hear Gabriel's trumpet first; so he may slide."

The school was organized, and its influence became so strong that the parson had to close his Sunday *doggery*.   He was also presented before the grand jury for running his transportation wagons on Sunday.

Tommie Ewing.—Mr. McCullagh had an ap-

pointment to start a school at a village on the
Ohio river. Two days before he reached the
place a distressing accident occurred. Two
little boys and girls were riding in a skiff,
when it was upset and they were drowned.
Their sudden death made a deep impression
on the hearts of the young and the old. In
his address he referred to the sad event, and
spoke of the uncertainty of life. He repeated
this stanza several times, until the children all
learned it:

> "My pulse is the clock of my life,
>   It tells me the moments are flying;
> It marks the departure of time,
>   And shows me how fast I am dying."

Just as he was starting away, a sunny-faced
boy took him by the hand and said, "I thank
you very much for your sermon; it has done
me good. I am determined to be ready when
my time comes. Tell me some good books to
read that will show me how to be a good boy."
This the missionary did, and, not long after,
he heard that Tommie Ewing had found Christ
and was a member of the church.

Nearly twenty years after this, Mr. McCullagh was on the cars near Chattanooga, Tennessee, when a gentleman came in, carrying a large bundle of books. In a conversation with him he learned that it was Thomas Ewing. The bundle contained Sunday-school books. He had not forgotten the stanza "My pulse is the clock of my life."

Bill Knox and the Mill School.—"I went to one of the poorest, darkest points in the state to organize a school," he writes. "Having lost my way, I saw a boy, without hat or shoes, sitting on a fence.

"'My boy, what is your name?'

"'Bill Knox,' replied he.

"'Can you tell me how far it is to Green's Mills?'

"'Yes; I reckon it's about three miles, but you can't find your way to it.'

"'Why?'

"''Cause there aren't any way to go.'

"'I am sorry, for it is ten o'clock now, and I have to be there by eleven.'

"'Are you the man what's going to make a Sunday-school to our mills?'

"'Yes.'

"'Wait till I tell dad, then;' and he ran into the field calling, 'Ho, dad, here's a man what is going to have something to the mills—going to make a Sunday-school there. I specs we had better show him the way.'

"'All right, Bill; me and the ole woman maybe'll be there too.'

"Mr. Knox came to the fence, and the missionary warmly accosted him: 'Mr. Knox, we are going to have a Sunday-school at the mills, and will be glad to have you come and bring your wife and children.'

"'All right; we will be there.'

"Bill and I started off, and got there ahead of them. There was seldom seen such a crowd. As soon as the school was organized, I invited any one who could not read, and wished to learn, to come up and take their places at my right. The first to come were old Knox and his wife; then came Bill and his four sisters, not one of whom could read. This school prospered, and they now have a brick church.

"Not long ago," adds the missionary, "a genteel-looking young man took me by the hand warmly and said, 'I have come thirty miles on a mule to see you, Mr. McCullagh, and now you don't know me.'

"'Yes, it is a fact I do not know you; but I can see so little of your face, I cannot be blamed: shaving does not seem to be in the fashion up here.'"

The stranger said he was Bill Knox, who showed the missionary to Green's Mills; that all of his family learned to read in that school, and that he was now superintendent of a large school in McClean county.

The poor people among whom Mr. McCullagh worked were very grateful, and would sometimes ask him, "Do you not expect some pay for that fine sermon?" "Yes; if you will all do as I tell you, that will be pay enough."

Some, however, did not deem this sufficient. One man made him a rocking-chair, which lasted thirty-five years. Another said, "Your pony is broken down; I have a good saddle-horse; you must use him for six months, and let your pony rest." Others gave him butter, eggs, fowls and fruit. These he accepted, so as not to wound the warm and grateful hearts of those who offered them.

Distinguished Men.—Mr. McCullagh was not only brought into contact with the poor and ignorant, but also with some of the most distinguished men in the country. He had among his personal friends governors of some of the states, presidents of railroad companies, of banks and colleges, judges of courts, and many of the most prominent ministers, of all denominations, in the United States. His acquaintance with President Andrew Jackson was of a very pleasant nature. He visited him at the Hermitage after " Old Hickory" had retired from public life. The ex-President gave him a letter of introduction to some personal friends. This letter was dated

HERMITAGE, June 27, 1856.

To William Donelson, Esq., Captain S. Donelson, and others of the neighborhood.

GENTLEMEN:—This will be handed to you by the secretary of The American Sunday-School Union, Mr. John McCullagh, a gentleman highly recommended, etc. He will make known to you the object of his visit.

Respectfully, your obedient servant,

A. JACKSON.

Hon. Alexander H. Stephens.—Mr. Stephens was one of the most remarkable and influential men in the South, on account of his great intellectual powers and the unblemished character of his private life. The story of his struggle against poverty and physical weakness, until he became one of the foremost men of his state, is a grand illustration of moral courage. He was a vice-president of The American Sunday-School Union, and just before his death had been arranging for the support of a missionary in the county in which he was born.

Mr. McCullagh always received a cordial welcome at "Liberty Hall." The secret of this interest was that when a poor country boy Mr. Stephens entered a Union Sunday-school.

In 1874 Mr. Stephens made an address to a large number of Sunday-school teachers and scholars who visited his grounds. Mr. Stephens stood on the east portico of his house, supported by his crutches, and described the influence of the Sunday-school upon his life as follows:

"Never before have I addressed an audience, large or small, upon topics relating exclusively not to things of this life, but to that higher life which is to come after.

"If I have not thus before spoken publicly upon such subjects, it has not been because I have not thought most intensely and profoundly upon them from my earliest youth. It is a source of high gratification for me to say to you all upon this occasion, and especially to these little boys, that the first awakening of such thoughts in my mind, as well as my first taste for general reading, was quickened and brought into active exercise in a Sunday-school.

"It was at the old Power Creek log meeting-house, not five miles from this place, more than half a century ago, that I became a pupil in what was known as a Union Sunday-school. The day I entered it was a great epoch in my life. It was in the latter part of the summer; and though but a small boy at the time, still I had to do such work on the farm as I was able to do during the week. This was picking cotton or peas, or going to mill, or other light work of like character. It was only at night, and by a pine-knot light, that I had any opportunity to study the lessons assigned me; and yet so deeply did I become interested in the

7

questions of the Union Catechism [Questions]
that two o'clock often found me poring over
the chapters of the Bible set apart for the next
Sunday's examination. To the impressions thus
made I am indebted in no small degree for my
whole future course in life, whether it has been
for good or for evil. If in the midst of any
evil that has marred that course there is anything good to be found, or anything worthy of
imitation, then it is due to that Sunday-school,
and to that great cause which you to-day cel-
ebrate with inspiring mottoes, banners and
music."

CHAPTER XIII.

THE OPPOSITION LINE.

In carrying on his work for The American Sunday-School Union, Mr. McCullagh met with great opposition. The following incidents illustrate his tact and perseverance in overcoming his opponents. He declares:

"It was hard work to be a Sunday-school missionary years ago. Then my field included the 'Pocket,' in southern Indiana, 'Egypt,' in southern Illinois, and southwestern Kentucky. I found violent opposers among the followers of Robert Dale Owen—the Flat-heads, Hardshells and Iron-jackets; indeed, all of them might be classed among the 'opposition line.' Of course the Bible-school was especially obnoxious to all such characters.

"At one time I was challenged by an eloquent advocate of woman suffrage, free-love theories, etc., to discuss sociology and the subject of Sunday-schools at a noted camp-ground. If I declined to meet him, he threatened to break up every Union school in my field. The challenge was accepted, and the time fixed for the discussion. An immense crowd was in attendance. I found the doctor knew nothing whatever about Sabbath-schools. As to his theory of sociology, it was a thoroughly-godless humanity, without any reverence for God, or truth to guide men and women in their conduct toward each other. He argued that there are no settled facts nor principles of common sense; he made marriage a partnership, to continue just as long as the interests of the partners required—'business on business principles.' It was a rehash of Plato, Sir Thomas More and John Stuart Mill. He made *this* hypothetical, *that* hypothetical, *everything* hypothetical.

"In closing my reply I told the temperance story of Johnny Hawkins, famous in the old Washingtonian temperance times, and confessed to a sort of logical sympathy with old Cæsar and his profound philosophy. It was the story of the negro debating society of Boston, in which old Cæsar, recently escaped from the tobacco-patch and corn-field, encounters the smooth-tongued Augustus, long in the classic halls of Cambridge, on the question ' Do the works of art or the works of nature have the most attraction for the human mind?' The grand defence of Cæsar against his voluble Cambridge opponent was the persistent refusal to allow his opponent's premises in the argument. So, as Augustus attempted a sublime description of the Boston State-house as a work of art that had many an attraction for the human mind, Cæsar called the gentleman to order, and demanded to know, ' Is not de Boston common de work ob nature, and derefore on our side? Where will de gentleman find a place to set his grand state-house?' ' But,' replies the indignant Augustus, ' will not de gentleman on de oder side, as de professors at Cambridge say, grant me de privilege to hypothecate de premises? Will he not gib me no premises?' ' I's got no premises for myself,' responds the imperturbable Cæsar, ' since I left my cabin in old Virginny. Go to work and buy you a premises, if you want one.' ' De gentleman misunderstands de point,' replies the smooth-tongued Augustus.

'I means de premises to hypothecate de argument. I's a right to hypothecate de premises, as, for instance, I say, Cæsar, suppose you over dar at Coon's grocery, for de sake ob argument.' 'But, nigger, I warn't dar,' replies the imperturbable Cæsar. 'I know you warn't dar,' replies the slick-tongued Augustus; 'but, jist to hypothecate de argument, I say, suppose you over at Coon's grocery.' 'Nigger, I warn't dar,' was Cæsar's dogged reply. 'I know, you fool, you warn't dar; but, as de professors at Cambridge say, we must hypothecate de argument. Now I say, only to hypothecate de argument, suppose you over dar at Coon's grocery.' 'You may,' cries the indignant Cæsar, 'pot-cake, if you please, or pound-cake, or pan-cake, or hoe-cake, if you please; but no man shall say dis nigger went to Coon's.'

"When the doctor arose to reply, the excitement was intense. Every man, woman and child was on his or her feet in a moment, exclaiming in thunder tones, 'I warn't dar,' 'I warn't dar.' I did my very best to quiet them so as to hear him out, but it was utterly impossible. 'No, sir,' they exclaimed; 'we have had enough, yes, *a little too much*, of such savage philosophy.' So the doctor picked up his hat and left in a hurry; when the president of the meeting remarked, 'Yes, he's gone, sure enough, and it's somewhat doubtful if he stops short of Pike's Peak.'

"The organization of six new Sabbath-schools was the result of the discussion. That New Harmony humbug of the Owens is dead and buried; the Flat-heads are all gone, and the Hard-shells and Iron-jackets are few and far between."

Uncle Johnny.—A Hard-shell preacher known as Uncle Johnny started an "opposition line." He charged that the missionary was a Britisher sent out by the government of old England to divide and ruin this country by establishing gospel-shops or Sunday-schools. I had organized them all around his churches. These gospel fires spread in every direction and swept everything before them; even his children and grandchildren deserted the "opposition line." This made him furious. He sent a challenge to debate "Sunday-schools and book-larning."

The challenge was accepted, the time fixed and the judges appointed. On reaching Big Creek, I found it over its banks and the bridge gone. I started up the creek, expecting to cross at Long's Mill, but found the water rushing over the dam like a young Niagara. Overwhelmed with sorrow and disappointment, I wept like a child at the very thought that Uncle Johnny would have such a grand triumph, and proclaim that he knew well enough that young chap wouldn't come to time.

After a full and thorough examination of the mill-dam and its surroundings, and having duly considered the dangers to be encountered, I determined to cross, and selected the upper part of the dam, where the current was not so swift. It was absolutely necessary that I should cross then and there, or fail to reach the camp-ground in time for the meeting. After committing myself and my loved ones at home, and the dear cause that I loved so much, to the care and keeping of my mother's God, I said to my faithful pony, "Now, Charry, go ahead for a long swim." She went in with a rush, but got fastened to a sunken tree about the middle of the dam. In trying to get clear of it the tree began to move, and down, down we floated, fastened in its branches. The pony seemed to realize the danger, and after several tremendous efforts got clear. The tree soon floated over the dam, and we reached the shore in safety.

A very large crowd were on the camp-ground. According to the programme, I spoke the first half hour. When Uncle Johnny arose to reply I noticed he was greatly excited. He commenced by saying, "My friends, when I left home I expected to make short work with this young chap and the gospel-shops; but—but—but when Brother Thomas told me how the chap had crossed the mill-dam, and described the miraculous escape he had, I came to the conclusion that he is in dead earnest; that he is honest, and is entitled to a martyr's crown; that the cause is a good one, although I have often denounced him and The American Sunday-School Union, calling them a pair of black sheep, etc.; but I was wrong, and take it all back." He then took my hand in both of his and exclaimed, "I am mighty glad, my brother, that you were not drowned, and may our Father in heaven bless you and the cause you so fearlessly stand up for.   I will never lay a feather in your way hereafter."

Then a good Methodist sister shouted, " Thank the Lord! I do believe Uncle Johnny has got religion!   Glory be to God!" and commenced singing

"Come, let us anew our journey pursue."

Such singing, shouting, hand-shaking and rejoicing I have never heard nor witnessed.   Perhaps I ought to add that the young missionary shouted and sang as loud as any Methodist on the camp-ground.   A glorious revival of religion followed.

The Shady and the Sunny Side.—The missionary organized a Sunday-school in a neighborhood called G——.   Among the scholars enrolled were twelve sons from one family, and seven boys and their little sister from another. The school made a fine start, and the prospect was bright.

A short time after, the missionary met a man, who addressed him in a very insulting manner: "I would like to know who gave you the authority to take my twelve sons into your Sunday-school."

"I had the best authority in the world; it was done at the request of their mother."

The man was very profane and abusive, and wound up his drunken tirade by saying, "I want you to understand, sir, that I am going to break up your old Sunday-school. Not one of my sons shall ever enter it again. Me and my boys will open the opposition line next Sunday."

He was true to his word, and on the next Sunday his house became the rendezvous for all the wicked people in the community. Liquor-drinking, gambling, dancing and all kinds of boisterous sports were the order of the day. This was kept up Sabbath after Sabbath; and during the week the young people were invited to come to his house on Sunday and have a good time. The little Sunday-school, however, continued to flourish in a quiet way.

About twenty years after, McCullagh again visited that section. As he looked up the road, he saw a man who was very much intoxicated riding toward him. The stranger could scarcely sit on his horse, and looked as though he would fall into the mud every moment. When he came up, his eyes were red and his face bloated.

"How are you, Mr. McCullagh? I haven't seen you for a long time. Don't you know me?"

"I think not."

"What! don't know me?" he muttered in a thick, stammering tone. "Don't you remember taking twelve boys into your Sunday-school years ago, and how the old man cussed you, and said he was going to start the 'opposition line,' and took all of us boys out?" He then began to curse and abuse his own father with fearful oaths. "Yes, the old man died a sot, and Bob is dead, and Sam, and George, and Will; all of the boys are in drunkards' graves. Mother died years ago of a broken heart, and you can see what I am. God bless you, old man; and I hope you will tell the people everywhere that the 'opposition line' don't pay."

The Sunny Side.—There is a bright side to

this sad story. We gave the dark side first. On entering the Sunday-school in a southern city, the superintendent grasped Mr. McCullagh's hand and continued to shake it until he thought the shaking would continue all day. " Very glad to see you, and I don't believe you remember me. I am one of the seven boys you enrolled in the Sunday-school at G——. We are all workers in the Sunday-school now, and our sister is a faithful teacher."

There is an interesting circumstance connected with this incident. In after years, when Mr. McCullagh was speaking in the New England states, the late Dr. John Todd questioned the size of these two families. Twelve children in one family seemed almost incredible. On his return to Kentucky, Mr. McCullagh got a number of certificates, sworn to before state officers, not only from families who had twelve children, but from some having fourteen, some sixteen and some eighteen children. These certified statements he sent on to the Rev. Dr. Todd and his New England friends.

CHAPTER XIV.

CO-WORKERS.

ENTHUSIASTIC about the Sunday-school work himself, McCullagh had the happy faculty of imparting his enthusiasm to others. The Sunday-school children in Kentucky felt that they too must help on the good cause. The various ingenious methods which they adopted to earn money are suggestive. Some of them had their missionary hens, turkeys and ducks, which were sold and the money saved for Sunday-school work. The boys sawed wood, baled shingles, and worked in the garden; the girls sewed, made carpet-rags and knitted socks.

Stuttering Willie.—One little girl in Henderson county knitted a pair of socks and sold them. She gave Mr. McCullagh the money to buy a Bible for some poor child. Soon after, he visited southern Illinois and organized a Sunday-school. While he was enrolling their names, he noticed a little boy who seemed very modest and bashful. He asked for his name.

The child seemed greatly embarrassed, and made several efforts to reply, but had an impediment in his speech; it was a great effort for him to stammer out, "My name is Stuttering Willie." The other boys came around him and said, "Go home, Willie, and stay there until you can learn to talk." Willie was an orphan, and the boys imposed on him. The little fellow was deeply wounded by these cruel words, and was ready to cry. Mr. McCullagh put his hand on the boy's head and said, "No, indeed; Willie is coming to Sunday-school every Sunday." At the close of the meeting he showed them the Bible that the little girl in Kentucky had bought, and told them he was going to leave it with their superintendent to give to the scholar who made the greatest progress during the year.

Three years after, he met the superintendent and asked him who received the Bible. "Why, that little orphan chap, 'Stuttering Willie.' He is the smartest boy I ever saw, and has almost broken himself of stammering."

The sequel to this incident is interesting.

Many years after, Mr. McCullagh was travelling on the Mississippi river. On the boat he noticed a man watching him very closely. Finally he sat down, and the man came and promenaded up and down before him, and steadily watched him. At last the gentleman said, "I beg your pardon, sir, for my apparent rudeness; but only at this moment am I certain that I know you. You are Mr. McCullagh, the Sunday-school man. I am the orphan boy whom they called 'Stuttering Willie.' Twenty-five years ago you placed your hand on my head and spoke kindly to me. That day was the turning-point in my life. I knew there was something in me, and determined that it should come out. I won the Bible you offered as a prize, and have it now in my travelling-bag. My business has prospered. I am now an officer in the church and a worker in the Sunday-school."

Rebecca Thomas' Ring.—When working down on the Cumberland river, Mr. McCullagh held a meeting to organize a school. After speaking of what Christ has done for us, he then considered what can we do for him. We can (1) speak for Jesus; (2) sing for Jesus; (3) work for Jesus; (4) give for his cause.

In speaking on the last point he said, "Many people have treasures laid away which they think are too precious to give even to the cause of Christ. They tell us that Martin Luther had a beautiful medal of Joachim, presented to him by the Elector of Brandenburg, which he prized very highly, and had hidden it away in his chest. Not long after, an urgent appeal was made to Luther for funds to aid an important Christian enterprise. He lamented that he was penniless. He soon remembered, however, that he had 'Joachim' hid in his chest. 'How can I give that up? What was Joachim made for, but to do good in the world?' He then went to the chest and exclaimed, 'Come forth, Joachim; why dost thou hide thyself? Dost thou not see how idle thou art? Come out and make thyself useful.' He then took out the medal and sent it forth on its mission, and Luther was all the happier. Our treasure pays best when cast into the imperishable mould of a good deed."

A collection was then taken up to purchase a

8

library for the school. The people were poor, and only a small amount was realized. When he was preparing to leave, Rebecca Thomas, a little girl, came up, and handing him a gold ring said, "Here is my Joachim. My mother gave me this ring, and I prize it very much; but I wish you to buy us some Sunday-school books with it." He reluctantly accepted it, · and promised to return the next Sabbath and bring the books.

During the week he met a Christian gentleman and told him about the ring. "Well," said the old man, "that is too bad." Putting his hand in his pocket he took out a ten-dollar gold piece and said, "Here, Brother McCullagh, take this and buy the books for them, and when you return give back her ring to the little girl."

When he returned, he saw Rebecca and handed her the ring: "Here is your ring, daughter; the Lord has opened the way to get the books."

She hung her head for a moment; then, with a brighter face, she looked up and said, "If my ring has gotten these books, and you still have it, I wish you to keep it and use it in the Sunday-school work. Maybe others will give something which they love, for the cause of Christ." She was firm in her refusal to take it.

Mr. McCullagh showed this ring and the ten-dollar gold piece, giving the history connected with them, in many Sunday-schools which he afterwards visited. He estimated that they brought into the treasury of The American Sunday-School Union more than fourteen thousand dollars. The society now owns the ring.* It is an active missionary: What a glorious harvest shall follow this noble act of self-sacrifice!

Emma J. Hill's Dollar.—On his regular visits to Nashville, Tenn., Mr. McCullagh addressed the Sunday-school of the Second Presbyterian Church. A little girl in that school was deeply impressed with his facts showing what children could do. She was afterwards taken very sick, and when at the point of death desired to make

---

* It is in the hands of the Rev. J. H. McCullagh, and its inspiring history is still stirring other hearts to make self-denying gifts to the Lord's work.—EDITOR.

her will. "I wish to leave it all for Christ." She had but one gold dollar. It was given to Mr. A. G. Adams, superintendent of the Sunday-school, and also a vice-president of The American Sunday-School Union. Mr. Adams took the dollar and attached it to a white card, and wrote on it, "Her legacy," "Her little all for Christ," "See that Jesus gets it all," and other beautiful expressions that she had used. He sent it to Mr. McCullagh.

This beautiful and touching story has been told from one end of the land to the other, and its influence has been wonderful. Mr. McCullagh calculated that it had been the means of raising seventeen thousand dollars for the Sunday-school work; and the end is not yet. How precious is the assurance "their works do follow them"!

Ida May Bowen.—On one of his visits to Albany, N. Y., a little girl named Ida May Bowen, nine years of age, heard one of his addresses in a Lutheran Sunday-school. She resolved to raise the money to start a Sunday-day-school. In the rear of their house was a little garden. She bought flower seeds and bulbous roots and planted them. When they blossomed, she made pretty little bouquets and sold them on the streets.

One day she asked Mr. Erastus Corning to buy some of her flowers. He said, "Why, child, what are you selling flowers for?"

"To organize a Sabbath-school in the South," she replied.

"What do you know about the South?"

"Mr. McCullagh has told us all about it."

He bought all that she had, and paid several times her price for them. She did not find many such customers as Mr. Corning was, and it took a long time to sell fifteen dollars' worth. She finally raised that amount, and Mr. McCullagh organized a school in a very needy place in Crittenden county, Ky., and called it the Mayflower Sunday-school.

The next three years she sold flowers and autumn leaves, and furnished the means to organize a school each year. When she was thirteen years of age she had organized four Mayflower schools, containing about four hundred members.

We have seen Ida's historic little flower

garden; it must have required great labor and skill to have produced such grand results.

Miss Charlotte Sprague, daughter of the Rev. Dr. Sprague, pastor of the Second Presbyterian Church, Albany, became interested in Mr. McCullagh's work. Although a confirmed invalid for years, her needle and deft fingers were ever busy. Now in her chair, then half reclining on her couch, she was weaving her love for destitute children into the very fabric of her handiwork.

At one time she held a fair in her father's house, for the sale of the beautiful articles she had made. The proceeds amounted to the handsome sum of two hundred dollars. Thus she worked on for years, until the summons came for her to rest from her labors and enter into the joy of her Lord. She earned enough money to organize some seventy Sunday-schools, containing about five thousand scholars.

These schools, as might be expected, planted by such loving hands, and nurtured by constant prayers, have been remarkably blessed. Several churches have grown out of them.

One of these schools was started in a very destitute place, where there was neither a church, Sunday-school nor day-school. The old log school-house had become an utter ruin. The missionary helped with his own hands to make it habitable, and put in rough temporary seats. This school was soon after blessed with a revival, in which about one hundred were converted, and a church was organized.

These heroic workers who, all unknown to fame, amid toil, pain and keenest suffering, take up daily and hourly burdens, and bear them for the good of others, for Jesus and his loved ones, shall be had in everlasting remembrance. "Give her of the fruits of her hands: and let her own works praise her in the gates."

Unknown Friend.—In 1880 Mr. McCullagh made an appeal for a missionary to labor in Virginia. This was responded to by a gentleman in "The Old Dominion," with a contribution of six hundred dollars, who signed his name as "Unknown Friend." The missionary was employed, and providentially located in the town where Unknown Friend resided. At this time, neither Mr. McCullagh nor the missionary knew who Unknown Friend was, or where he lived.

A young minister was the missionary, and without being aware that he was working right under the eye of his patron, he commenced a vigorous Sunday-school campaign.

Unknown Friend was a good Methodist brother, and had frequent conversations with the worker, and sometimes accompanied him in the work, but never gave a hint that he was supporting the missionary. In this way he thoroughly measured the man and the value of the work. In a short time he was so well pleased with his investment that he gave six hundred dollars more to employ another missionary. Being a man with a family, such contributions could only be made with great personal sacrifice. But many of God's people have learned by experience that "it is more blessed to give than to receive."

Many Sabbath-schools contributed nobly to the cause; among them are Bellefield Union School, Pittsburgh; School Street Sabbath-school, Allegheny; Madison Avenue Reformed

School, Albany; Brown Memorial and Westminster schools, Baltimore.

The foregoing instances are representatives of the great army of helpers throughout the country who co-operated with him in the blessed work. Many who were wealthy gave their hundreds and thousands, many who were poor giving small sums. They were scattered among all the churches; Baptist, Congregationalist, Dutch Reformed, Episcopal, Friends, Lutheran, Methodist, Presbyterian; and many who could not be classed with any denomination, gave from the impulse of philanthropy, believing that Bible instruction for neglected children was one of the best possible investments.

CHAPTER XV.

THE FIELD WIDENS.

In 1852 Mr. McCullagh's success in active missionary work was so marked that in addition to this service, he was appointed to superintend others. For ten long years he had stood solitary and alone, the only Sunday-school missionary in the great and growing commonwealth of Kentucky. He now visited the larger towns in the state, to awaken increased interest in the Sunday-school cause, and to collect funds to employ new missionaries, and train them for effective work.

He made regular visits to Louisville, Lexington, Winchester, Bardstown, Frankfort, Danville, Springfield, Nicholasville, Bloomfield, Midway, Shelbyville, Owensboro', Lebanon, Bowling Green and many other places. He received such liberal contributions that, in 1856, he writes, " I now have twenty assistants planting the Sunday-school banner in destitute places." Other states were gradually added to his care, until he had the supervision of the society's field work in the South. Being an excellent judge of human nature, he selected competent, consecrated men for the work. Some of these continued in the employ of the society for thirty years, being among its most successful missionaries. He visited them on their fields of labor, encouraged and assisted them.

He gives the following illustrations of the nature of this work :

"During the year 1878 I have visited my old field, where forty years ago we set up our banner. What progress has been made ! What a rich harvest has been and is still being reaped ! The orange tree, with its large ripe fruit, its advancing young fruit and its buds and blossoms on the same branches, is a fitting representation of what we have seen in our Bible schools.

"I spent several weeks with Brothers H. and R. in the mountains of Kentucky. Our journey was really a triumphal march through a number of counties. The meetings were large and interesting, comprising all ages, from the little Sunday-school scholar to the old patriarch of ninety-one, all wanting to hear and learn more about Jesus and the great salvation.

"I could not help noticing how, at every town and neighborhood, the people came out to greet our missionaries and grasp their hands, expressing joy and delight at seeing them once more, with such expressions and exclamations as, 'Our school is getting on finely;' 'We have had a glorious revival;' 'Our school has more than doubled since you were here last;' 'Mighty glad to see you back again;' 'We are all going nine miles to attend your meetings next Sunday at Fighting Creek.'"

One of the missionaries in Kentucky wrote:

"In August I accompanied Rev. John McCullagh, superintendent of our work in the South, on a mountain trip, which resulted in great profit to the good cause in that region. Our first stopping-place was at Livingston, Rock Castle county, Rock Castle river, where in 1872 I planted a Sunday-school. It was casting bread upon the waters, which has been gathered after many days. The Spirit revealed his presence and power in our meeting there at night; and about twenty professed their desire for salvation. We left the meeting in the hands of the brethren; and the final result was, seventy professed faith in Christ. Our next objective point was forty-five miles out in the mountains in Knox county, where we held meetings for a few days with the Fighting Creek Sunday-school. As the immediate result nearly twenty professed like precious faith in Christ and asked to be organized into a church. Thus, in all our trip and labors we were blessed and made to rejoice in the success of the Lord's work. We are persuaded that the planting of Sunday-schools at these points was the beginning of those gracious seasons of revival and conversion—the result, under God, of the prayerful and faithful teaching and labor of those who had a heart and mind for the work."

Having such a leader to help and encourage them, one who would be satisfied only with their best efforts, the results in the South, considering the number of men employed, have been phenomenal in the religious history of our times.

Getting Contributions.—In order to secure the funds necessary to extend the work, Mr. McCullagh made regular visits to Pittsburgh, Harrisburg, Albany (N. Y.), Louisville, Nashville, Philadelphia, Baltimore and New York, and tours through New England. In these cities his direct, forcible and earnest pleas in behalf of Sunday-school Union missions always won for the cause the sympathy and support of intelligent business men. He was ever warmly welcomed in the pulpit, on the platform and in the counting-house. Many large-hearted Christians, enlisted in giving to this work by his appeals, continued their hearty support year by year for more than forty years.

In all these places he made many life-long friends. It would be a pleasure to give sketches of this noble band of contributors, many of whom have gone to their reward, but it would require a volume to contain even their names. These contributors he affectionately called " God's jewels," and ever held them in loving remembrance.

As a collector of funds, he had but few equals. On one occasion he entered the office of a friend in Louisville. The clerk said, "Here is Mr. McCullagh."

"All right," responded the proprietor, hastily getting out his pocket-book; "I am like Davy Crockett's coon; I will come down without being smoked."

A good old brother in Pittsburgh, who has since gone home to rest, said, "Will I give a contribution to the Sunday-school work? Indeed I will. I never saw such a man as you, Brother McCullagh; you could talk a bird off a bush to come and get into your hand."

At one time the society directed him and one of their other agents to canvass a western city. The first day Mr. McCullagh was a few dollars behind his colleague in the amount collected, and the good brother was disposed to boast over his success. The next day Mr. McCullagh called on a gentleman who gave him one hundred dollars. That night, on comparing notes, his colleague was far behind; and seeing the subscription for one hundred dollars, he said, "I saw that gentleman yesterday and he only gave me thirty dollars, and to-day he gives you a hundred. I will not work against you. I leave on the next train, and you must finish the canvass."

He was earnest, persistent and enthusiastic in collecting. Said a friend to him once, "I do not see how you stand this begging money. It is the hardest, most trying and disagreeable work in the world. People will get so they will shun you, as if you were a constable or a tax collector."

"I do not beg for money," he replied. "I only state our cause, and leave it with their consciences to give or not. If the Lord's work needs money and his people have it, I only do my duty to him and them when I tell them of it. When I show that 'the Lord hath need of them,' they will respond."

He often received contributions from persons who were not members of any church. These he called "Noah's carpenters;" and he would sometimes say to them, "I am sorry to place you among Noah's carpenters."

"We do not understand what you mean," they replied.

"Well, Noah's carpenters helped to build the ark, but they would not go into it. The flood came, the ark floated off, and they were drowned. You are helping us to get people into the ark of safety, and you have not gone in yourself. Delay is dangerous. When I come back next year, I hope to hear a better account of you."

This statement caused many of them to consider the "great question." This arrow at a venture, under the blessing of God, was the means of bringing one young man into the church, who became a vice-president of the society and noted for his benevolence.

At the close of the war, when the southern states were impoverished and ruined, McCullagh's efforts for their relief were incessant. He visited old friends whom he had known in the days of affluence, and now found them in a pitiful condition. We will not describe the sad state of things during those dark days; words would fail us. His heart was stirred within him. He hastened North, and in the leading cities described what he had seen. The response was noble and Christ-like. The society was enabled to furnish books by the ten thousand volumes to a people who were heart-sick and

9

starving for the bread of life. The old regime had fallen; the relation of master and slave had ceased to exist. Four million of slaves were suddenly free, and a chaotic condition seemed likely to ensue.

In this critical and dangerous period The American Sunday-School Union rendered most important service to our country. Indeed it is regarded by some as the fairest and most glorious page in her noble history.

CHAPTER XVI.

DURING THE WAR.

KENTUCKY being a border state, and having soldiers from both armies constantly on her soil, the feeling of dread and suspense paralyzed almost all interests. Mr. McCullagh went right along with his Sunday-school work as though peace was reigning. Though partisan hate was, perhaps, more bitter in Kentucky than in any other state, his course was so wise that he had the cordial good will of both sides. His sense of security was sometimes a great danger to him, as the following will illustrate.

He went to Danville, Ky., to visit his daughter, who was attending the Caldwell Female Institute. Central Kentucky at that time was in terror on account of the extraordinary movements of General John Morgan. Danville was a strong Union town, and when it was known that Morgan was likely to capture the place, a number of Union men who had incurred the displeasure of the Confederates thought it wise to flee to Louisville for safety.

While on his visit there, Morgan's men in large numbers got between Danville and Louisville, and all communication was cut off. Mr. McCullagh determined to start for Louisville, but his friends endeavored to dissuade him, saying that he could not get through the lines. Yet he would not stop on account of difficulties. There were several teachers in the Institute from New England, and on the morning he was to leave, they, and the friends of the Union men who had fled to Louisville, brought him about a hundred letters, which they asked him to mail when he reached Louisville. He took the letters, hired a conveyance, and started on his perilous journey.

When he had gone about twenty miles, he saw a cloud of dust rising in the distance, and in a few moments about one hundred cavalry men came in sight. They dashed up and said, "Where are you going?"

"I am on my way to Louisville."

"Where are you from?"

"I left Danville this morning."

"What are you trying to get through our lines for?"

"I have business in Louisville."

"Have you a pass from General Morgan?"

"No, sir."

"What have you in that valise?"

"I have shirts, handkerchiefs, some sermons and a few other things."

"Empty it and we will see."

As he was bending over to unlock the valise, Captain G. dashed up, and shaking hands cordially with him said, "How are you, Mr. McCullagh? Still on your Sunday-school work in time of war?" Turning to his men, he said, "Boys, this is old man McCullagh, the Sunday-school preacher. You have no time to fool with him. He is all right. Forward, march;" and away they galloped.

When he reached Louisville he met one of the Union refugees, and handed him some half dozen letters.

"Mr. McCullagh, did you bring these letters from Danville through Morgan's lines?"

"Yes, sir; and a big pile of them for people all through the North. I met a hundred soldiers, and they wanted to see everything in my bag."

"What!" exclaimed the man, bursting into tears; "if you had opened that bag, they would have hanged you without delay. According to the rules of war you were a spy, and guilty of death. Spies receive no mercy."

He replied, "Well, the good Lord saved me this time, and I will carry no more letters for anybody while this war lasts."

His name was also a great protection for his missionaries. One of these was a strong Union man, and had a great horror of John Morgan. It so happened that the missionary rode a very fine horse, and in going to an appointment had to pass the Confederate outpost. The horse was too great a temptation for the soldiers, and straightway the missionary was carried under guard to General Morgan.

A sharp colloquy followed.

"Where are you going, sir?"

"To start a Sunday-school at Goose Creek."

"A Sunday-school! That is a likely story. You look like a Sunday-school man. They don't ride that kind of horse. Not much! Got anything to show?"

"Yes, sir; here is my commission, signed by our secretary and countersigned by Rev. John McCullagh, superintendent."

Morgan took the commission and read it slowly. "I don't know that other chap; only old Mac; I know him. He is the prophet, apostle and high priest of Sunday-schools. I heard him when I was not knee-high to a duck. Can you sing?"

"Yes, sir."

"Go at it then."

With a slight tremor in his voice he began to sing Sunday-school songs. It was a picture for an artist. The missionary singing for dear life; the rude surroundings of the camp and army; the officers sitting on their horses; rough, hard men gathered in groups, leaning on their rifles. The charm of music and the power of association brought back home and fireside, Sunday-school and the memory of other days. Tears bedimmed the eyes of those strong men. Suddenly Morgan's voice rang out, "Boys, this man is all right. Old Mac picks out the right kind. Let him go."

Mr. McCullagh went to Wheeling during the war, and told how the missionaries were allowed to pass through the lines of both armies. Good old Dr. Weed, of blessed memory, sat in the pulpit with him, and exclaimed, "Thank God! The American Sunday-School Union is the GOLDEN LINK that binds the North and the South together."

Going North and South every year, McCullagh saw the trouble and sorrow that wrung the hearts of the people in those sad times. It was often his privilege to help those in distress.

Blind Ben.—In 1864, when travelling on a steamboat, he learned that a number of wounded soldiers were on board. He went below, and looking at the unfortunate men said, "Are there any of my old Sunday-school boys down here?" A young man replied, "Mr. McCullagh, come this way, please."

He went to the soldier, and found that a handkerchief was tied over both eyes. "I am so glad to hear your voice once more. I knew it was you, Mr. McCullagh, the moment you spoke. I am Ben B. You entered my name in the Pleasant Grove School, in Davis county, Ky. *Alas! I am stone blind* for life. A ball entered one of my eyes and destroyed the other also. You must now call me Blind Ben. I remember your Sunday-school address well. You told us all to memorize the fifty-third chapter of Isaiah, the fifty-first Psalm, and the third chapter of the Gospel by John; and you told us never to forget the sixteenth verse of that chapter, as it contained the substance of the whole Bible; and that the fifty-first Psalm was about the best prayer ever written. Alas! these sightless balls can never see you in this world; but I hope to see you up yonder, where we shall all see the King in his beauty."

Only two days before his death a gentleman from a distant city called to see him. He said, "I have not seen your father for twenty-five years. When I last saw him it was during the war, and I was in prison; he came to see us, brought us a box of good books to read, and loaned us money. I shall never forget him."

"Then shall the King say unto them on his right hand, Come, ye blessed of my Father, inherit the kingdom prepared for you from the foundation of the world. . . . I was sick, and ye visited me; I was in prison, and ye came unto me."

CHAPTER XVII.

As superintendent of the Southern District, Mr. McCullagh's duties required him to make frequent tours throughout the country, to present the claims of The American Sunday-School Union. Of this branch of his work he wrote, "I have addressed Sunday-school anniversaries and general Sunday-school meetings, from Charleston, South Carolina, to Bangor, Maine, and from Richmond to Minneapolis; sometimes having from six to eight appointments each Sabbath, and several during the week."

On some of these tours he was accompanied by Stephen Paxson, Chidlaw and other veterans in the work. In Philadelphia, New York and other cities the largest churches were filled to hear them. Mr. McCullagh regarded the story of Stephen Paxson's life as the most telling illustration of the society's work.

138

The pulpit and platform were Mr. McCullagh's throne. At the sight of a large audience his eye flashed, and he seemed like a war-horse impatient for the charge. At a meeting in Washington city, over which a judge of the Supreme Court presided, with the President of the United States and other distinguished officials on the platform, he manifested the same tact and adaptation that he used before a crowd of ignorant men in their shirt-sleeves, in the back woods of Kentucky.

His addresses were filled with facts, which he brought out with great pathos and power. Possessing action in a high degree, his nervous, clear-cut sentences attracted and held the attention of the most indifferent auditors. Some Sunday-schools he addressed regularly for more than forty years, and the day of his coming was hailed with pleasure by old and young.

L. Milton Marsh, secretary of the society's work for New York, gives this instance : " The fruits of personal labors of our missionaries are not confined to distant fields. Some years since, our faithful co-laborer Rev. J. McCullagh gave a missionary address to one of the prominent churches of an adjoining city, which had given largely for our work. As the result, they were stirred up to organize a mission Sunday-school in their own town, which has been a great success, and the labor of sustaining it proved to be of great value to the life of the church. The two schools now have about two thousand five hundred members. One of the officers of the church school said, 'We are greatly indebted to The American Sunday-School Union for the impetus given to our church by Mr. McCullagh's stirring words.'"

Instead of giving any of his addresses in full, we present some extracts from them, from which a general idea of their character may be derived. On one occasion, after giving some pointed incidents from his missionary experience, he said, "We are often asked, 'How can you account for such wonderful results?' There are several reasons for it. The Sunday-school missionary, unlike many other Christian workers, leaves permanent organizations, self-supporting, self-conducting, self-instructing, that will live after he has left them, to confer on other neighborhoods similar blessings, as they often become the parents of other schools, the germs of evangelical churches and nurseries of heaven.

"Again, we have no story to tell but the story of the cross. The motto and key-note of The American Sunday-School Union for half a century has been 'Jesus only.' There is in the Vatican gallery at Rome one of the grandest of all the creations of art—the famous painting of Raphael representing the transfiguration on the mount. Two sets of figures are to be seen; the conception of that wonderful and almost inspired painter. One is the prostrate disciples, the hovering figures of Moses and Elijah on the mountain-top amid a halo of glory; while on the back-ground or plains below are the convulsed demoniac, the anxious father, the perplexed disciples and the sympathizing crowd. The other is the central figure of Christ, glowing with such transcendent radiance that all other forms are lost, so that we can see no man save Jesus only. The cross is the mightiest power in the universe. Jesus is the head of all things to his Church. For another year, and for another fifty years, shall we not in his name set up our banners, and take as our motto 'Jesus only'?

'There is no name so sweet on earth,
No name so sweet in heaven.'

In his cross is the power that conquers and draws us together.

"After the battle of Manassas, a Federal soldier lay mortally wounded. A Confederate came by, and the dying man asked him if he would pray for him. The answer was, 'I am sorry, I don't pray for myself; but I will move you to a more comfortable place, and bring you some water.'

"Afterwards a Virginia cavalry man passed by. The dying soldier repeated his request and asked his enemy to make a prayer. The trooper said he would try. He knelt down by his side and began. As he prayed the wounded man drew closer and closer to him, and with his last remaining strength partially raised himself until his head touched the shoulder of the petitioner. When the prayer was ended, he was dead—dead with his head resting on the bosom of his late foe. The power of the cross made them one in Christ Jesus. I doubt not these two men will sing together the song of redeeming love. Even here on earth we feel it good to sing

> 'Blest be the tie that binds
> Our hearts in Christian love.'

*   *   *   *   *   *

"All evangelical denominations are benefited and built up by our Union work; hence we have the sympathy and co-operation of all. At an annual meeting of one of the leading denominations of North Carolina, not long ago, a historical sketch was read, in which the following statement was made : 'Nearly all the great and good work accomplished in the bounds of this body in the cause of Sunday-schools is justly attributable to the efficient agency of The American Sunday-School Union.'

"Again, in thousands of neighborhoods there must be Union schools or none. A correspondent writes, 'In thirteen counties lying west of the Blue Ridge there are five hundred Bible-schools, and more than four hundred of them are Union schools. This part of the country owes a great debt to The American Sunday-School Union.'"

*   *   *   *   *   *

The Missionaries.—Describing its missionaries and their work, he eloquently added: "What a wonderful regenerating power there is in Sabbath-school work! Corey, Paxson, Chidlaw, Upson, Lewis, Legarè and others are now beyond the fifties, yet they renew their youth like the eagles; they run and are not weary, they walk and are not faint. I think they will all die young men, and then begin immortal youth.

"What a long procession of Christians, patriots, heroes and statesmen will walk the narrow road from our Sabbath-schools, long after these veteran missionaries have unbuckled the sword of the conflict and gone home to rest!

"'Almost up, almost up!' was the cry of a wounded sergeant, as they laid him down on the battle-field, and watched tenderly his dying struggles.

"'Where did they hit you, sergeant?'

"'Almost up.'

"'No! sergeant, but where did the ball strike you?'

"'Almost up,' was the reply.

"'But, sergeant, you do not understand; where are you wounded?'

"Turning back the cloak which had been thrown over the wound, he showed the upper arm and shoulder, mashed and mangled with a shell. Looking at this wound, he said, 'That is what did it. I was hugging the standard to my blouse, and making for the top. I was almost up, when that ugly shell knocked me over. If they had let me alone a little longer—two minutes longer—I should have planted the colors on the top. Almost up, almost up!'

"The fight and the flag held all his thoughts. And while his ear was growing dull in death, with a flushed face and a look of ineffable regret he was repeating, 'Almost up, almost up!'

"Beloved comrades in the army of King Jesus, let this be our cry on the battle-field, and our joyful shout in death.

    *   *   *   *   *   *

"Will you allow me to give you a fact from my field? We often talk and think as if per-

10

secution and trials for Christ and his cause belonged to a past age. Such, however, is not the case.

"Let me tell you about Lucy L., the infidel's daughter. Several years ago I addressed a Sunday-school in Kentucky that you had supplied with a library. My subject was the 'Earthly House,' 'whose foundation is in the dust' (Job 4 : 19). I spoke of the eyes as the windows, the mouth as the door, the ears as the side-doors, the hands as the keepers or servants, the conscience the watchman, the soul the inhabitant. I spoke of its great value from its great cost, 'For ye are bought with a price: therefore glorify God in your body, and in your spirit, which are God's' (1 Corinthians 6 : 20), of self-consecration of eyes for Jesus, of mouth, tongue, hands, feet, soul and body—all for Christ. I spoke of the martyrs who would even die for Jesus.

"At the close of the meeting a young lady came and whispered, 'I will do it.'

"'Do what?' I inquired.

"'Give all to Jesus. He gave himself for me.'

"About two months after this it was whispered that the infidel's daughter was among the saints. A wonderful change in dress, in manner and even in countenance was noticed. As long as she attended the Sunday-school her father did not seem to care; but when he heard that a church was about to be organized, and that his daughter was likely to cast in her lot with such 'poor trash,' as he called them, he raved and stormed like a madman. He was proud of his only daughter. She was the brightest gem in his handsome home. He called her into his study, and inquired about the whole matter. She frankly told him all. He exclaimed, in a passionate voice, 'Do I understand you to say that for these ignorant people you will give up everything? If so, you must give up either your home and your father, or your religion.'

"She replied, 'I will give up all for Jesus.'

"'Do you intend to join the church?' he inquired.

"'Yes, father.'

"'Well, it comes to this: you can give up him whom Voltaire called a 'wretch,' or me.

Unless you give up this foolish idea, you cannot remain in my house; and henceforth I am your father only in name.'

"It is now Jesus, or father. There she stood, clothed with the mantle of a new and heavenly faith; its light shining in her broken heart and playing over her pale face. With martyr-like firmness she said, 'Jesus.'

"She gave up all for him, and took a little school as a means of support. A short time time afterward her step became slow, her form wasted, her eye hollow, and her cheek sunken. In a few months Lucy L. was on her death-bed. The day before she died she sent for her father.

"He came; but was cold, heartless, and as immovable as the rock of Gibraltar.

"She said, 'Father, I will soon have a home, a happy home, a heavenly home, where I will set a light in the window to guide you to the mansions of glory.'

"The next day a few Christian friends gathered around her bed and sang,

'Jesus, lover of my soul.'

Her face was angelic, her language rapturous, and that log cabin was the gate of heaven. They then sang,

> 'Rock of ages! cleft for me,
> Let me hide myself in thee.'

At its close they heard one word—the last. It was Jesus. Other than mortal eyes might have seen a chariot of glory come sweeping by, to bear Lucy L. to her heavenly home. Will the whole congregation please unite in singing those two precious stanzas:

> 'Rock of ages! cleft for me,
> Let me hide myself in thee;
> Let the water and the blood
> From thy wounded side that flowed,
> Be of sin the perfect cure;
> Save me, Lord! and make me pure.

> 'While I draw this fleeting breath,
> When mine eyelids close in death,
> When I rise to worlds unknown,
> And behold thee on thy throne,
> Rock of ages! cleft for me,
> Let me hide myself in thee.'

*   *   *   *   *   *

"'Oh, Sunday-school worker,' he continued, with feeling, as every eye was moistened, 'be faithful, be earnest, in this blessed cause. You know not what glorious results shall crown your labors.'

"In one of our schools was a teacher named Mrs. Long, who taught the young men's Bible-class. This class was composed of thirteen young men. She not only taught faithfully, but prayed without ceasing for the conversion of her scholars. She became the honored instrument in bringing twelve of them into the ark of safety.

"'All in but one,' she said, and she continued to pray for that one.

"On a wet, disagreeable Sabbath morning, her husband remarked, 'My dear, Clear Creek is over its banks, and I suspect the road is impassable beyond the bridge; so you can't go to Sunday-school to-day.'

"She replied that she had not missed a single Sabbath in five years, and felt that she must go that day and see Dave Nelson, for she had been praying for him all the week.

"She went and found her entire class present. When the school closed, Dave whispered, 'Please remain a little while; I wish to

talk with you.' He said that he had joined
the army, and his company were to leave for
the front the next day. He asked her to pray
for him.

" She answered, 'Dave, I have been praying
for you all the week.'

" In the conversation which followed she led
him to Jesus the Lamb of God, which taketh
away the sin of the world. In the ardor of
his first love, he exclaimed, 'Jesus is indeed
precious to me.'

"A few months later Dave Nelson was leading a charge in the bloody battle of Chicka-
mauga, and fell mortally wounded. When the
surgeon came around to care for the wounded, he examined Dave and said, 'We can't do
anything for this poor boy; he will die in a
little while.'

- "'Yes, you can,' said the dying boy. 'Open
my knapsack, and get out my books.'

" They got out a little Bible and a copy of
' The Great Question,' by Dr. H. A. Boardman,
in which was written, 'To David Nelson, from
his Sunday-school teacher.'

" He then gave them Mrs. Long's address,

and requested them to send the books to her, and write her that by coming to Sunday-school that rainy Sunday she had led him to the cross; and that Jesus, the dear Saviour, was with Dave Nelson in his sufferings. When he reached heaven he would be waiting at the gate for Mrs. Long, and would take her by the hand and bring her to Christ, and say, 'Precious Saviour! she brought me to thee.

"Oh, workers for Jesus, think of the cordial welcome you shall have when you reach the land of glory!

> 'They are waiting for our coming,
>   Watching on the other shore;
>   Waiting to receive the ransomed,
>   When the storms of life are o'er.
>
> 'Watching by the shining portals
>   Of our Father's mansion fair;
>   They will strike their harps of glory!
>   They will bid us welcome there.'"

CHAPTER XVIII.

PERSONAL CHARACTERISTICS.

Mr. McCullagh was of medium height, somewhat stout in frame, with strong, prominent features, and well-balanced mental and vital temperament in his constitution. We do not represent him as a perfect man. He was intense, earnest, and possessed the faults usually found in good people of this composition. Whatever his hands found to do he did with his might; his zeal rendered him impatient when confronted by delays and obstacles, and only increased his determination to overcome the difficulties. There were but few things which he took for granted, except intuitive truths, mathematical demonstrations, and the word of God.

He would not sign his name to any paper until he had carefully read every word. He believed strongly in the corrupting power of sin in the human heart, and from the many sad illustrations which he had seen of its power, he

153

hesitated to put confidence in untried persons; but when he was once convinced that a man was true and honorable, it mattered not what disasters should befall him, or how thick calumnies and evil report gathered around the once fair name, he never deserted a friend in misfortune or even in disgrace. We will enumerate a few of the leading points of his character, and in this way may be able to disclose the secret of his success; so that some of his young friends may be benefited in cultivating and imitating these qualities.

I. STRONG RELIGIOUS CONVICTIONS.

It was contrary to his nature to do anything by halves. Whatever he thought worth doing, he spared neither pains nor labor to do thoroughly. This principle was carried into his religious life.

After thorough examination of the Bible, he was convinced that it was the inspired word of God; and its precepts demanded as implicit obedience and respect as an audible command from Jehovah. He believed the great body of theology, as held by orthodox evangelical Christians, to be as true and permanent as the law of gravitation and the axioms in geometry. When he realized that he was a sinner, both by nature and continued transgression, and saw the mercy and love of God manifested in the death of Christ, he confessed his sins, accepted the offer of pardon, and consecrated his life, his all, to the God of mercy and love.

In witness of this great transaction, he wrote a document entitled "A Form of my Covenant with God," and put it away among his private papers, where it was found after his death. This covenant is long and solemn. It was repeatedly renewed through life. Some of the dates of renewal are January, 1833, June, 1838, January, 1841.

We give some extracts from it:

"Eternal and unchangeable Jehovah, the great Creator of heaven and earth, and adorable Lord of angels and men, I desire, with deepest humiliation and abasement of soul, to fall at this time in thine awful presence, and earnestly pray that thou wouldst penetrate my very heart with a suitable sense of thine unutterable glories. Trembling may justly take hold upon me when I a sinner presume to lift up my head to thee; presume to appear in thỳ presence on such an occasion as this. Who am I, O Lord God, or what is my father's house, that I should speak of this, and desire that I may be one party in a covenant, when thou, the King of kings, art the other!

"But, O Lord, great as is thy majesty, so great also is thy mercy. If thou wilt hold covenant with any of thy creatures, thine exalted nature must stoop infinitely low. I know that through Jesus, the Son of thy love, thou condescendest to visit sinful mortals. I come therefore, through thy Son, and trusting in his righteousness. I acknowledge I have been a great transgressor. My sins have reached unto the heavens. God, be merciful to me a sinner. Remember not against me my transgressions. I bring back to thee those powers and faculties which I have alienated from thy service. Receive, I beseech thee, thy poor revolted creature.

"With the utmost solemnity I make this surrender of myself to thee. Hear, O heavens, and give ear, O earth: I avouch the Lord this

day to be my God; I avouch and declare myself this day to be one of his covenant children. Hear, O Lord, and record it in the book
of thy remembrance that henceforth I am entirely thine. I would not merely dedicate unto
thee some of my powers or some of my possessions, or all of that I have for a certain
time; but I would be thine, wholly thine, for-
ever.

"Trusting in thy name and grace, I bid de-
fiance to sin and the power of hell. I desire
to spend the remainder of my days in the way
that shall effectually promote thy honor and
glory. I leave, O Lord, to thy management
and direction all I possess and all I wish, to be
disposed of as thou desirest; contentedly re-
solving to submit my will to thine. Use me,
O Lord, as the instrument of thy glory and
honor, and for the benefit of the world in which
I dwell.

"Grant that, through life and in my dying
moments and in the near prospect of eternity,
I may remember these my engagements with
thee, and may employ my latest breath in thy
service. And do thou, Lord, when thou seest

the agonies of dissolving nature upon me, remember this covenant too, even though I may be incapable of recollecting it.

"Heavenly Father, look with pitying eye upon me; place thine everlasting arms underneath me for support; put strength and confidence into my departing spirit, and receive me into the embrace of thy love.

"When I am numbered with the dead, if this memorial should chance to fall into the hands of any surviving friends, may it be the means of making serious impressions on their minds. May they read it not only as my language but as their own, and learn to love and fear the Lord God."

It may be well to observe here that all of the prayers which stood recorded in this document for more than half a century were answered. He was used as the honored instrument in bringing many to Christ. His latest breath was spent in prayer. The everlasting arms were around him. He passed away from earth to heaven without pain or sickness. The principles expressed in this covenant governed his Christian life. He was a diligent student of the Bible all his life, and read it regularly in private and in family devotions.

While he firmly held to the doctrines of the church in which he was reared, his sympathy and love embraced all of God's people. He had but little patience with denominational bigotry and sectarian exclusiveness. Believing that all evangelical churches hold much in common and differ only on non-essentials, he regarded it as both foolish and wrong to emphasize these minor points so as to produce bitterness and estrangement. He said, "We all have the same God and Father, the same Bible; we are all sinners saved by grace; we are all trying to reach the same heaven. Why should we spend our strength in fighting each other? Are there not in every church eloquent ministers, faithful missionaries and many noble, consecrated men and women? Does not God honor them all with the presence and power of his Spirit? Who has a monopoly of the word of God or his free Spirit? Let us beware how we oppose each other, lest haply we be found fighting against God."

He was firmly convinced that united Christian effort was irresistible, and regarded the work of the Bible Society and The American Sunday-School Union as an illustration of the point, and as a prophecy of good things yet to come. He was grieved to see that in some places the tendency of the times was to draw the denominational lines tighter, so as to exclude Union work. Why should this be done at a time when from eight to ten million children and youth in our country were not receiving religious instruction, and when Union and interdenominational effort was the only practicable and successful method of reaching most of them?

On one occasion, after addressing a large audience in a Virginian city, quite a number of persons came forward to speak to him. It seems that they had a dispute among themselves as to which church he belonged. One gentleman said, "I know from his fire and enthusiasm that he is bound to be a Methodist."

"No, sir," answered his friend; "there is too much Calvinism about him to be a Methodist. He is a Baptist."

A third one remarked, "Both of you brethren are mistaken. I know from his dignity and good taste that he is an Episcopalian."

Another said, "There is too much Scotch and Shorter Catechism about him for him to be anything but a Presbyterian."

He replied to them, "Well, brethren, I feel greatly complimented to be claimed by you all. I help all of the churches by my work, but I will not tell you to which regiment of the King's army I belong."

While he was conscious of the powers he possessed, and feared not the face of man, in things relating to God he was as humble as a child. When he erred, with tears of penitence and prayers of confession he sought forgiveness.

II. WILL POWER.

His perseverance and will power were remarkable. After carefully considering an undertaking and devising means for accomplishing it, seldom did he fail. Even though success did not come, he intermitted his efforts only in order to devise more powerful methods for its accomplishment.

11

One little incident will illustrate the influence of this quality of his character. He planted a strawberry-bed in his garden. The plants were growing beautifully, but were attacked by insects and destroyed. Having taken great pleasure and pride in his garden, he secured other plants and tried again. These were likewise destroyed. Nothing daunted, he tried again and again until the bed had been replanted twenty-five times, and victory crowned his efforts. When urged to give up the apparently hopeless contest, he replied, "No, indeed; that bug does not crawl that can whip me out. It is not my doctrine to give up what I undertake." This same determination to conquer, he exhibited in the great as well as in the small matters of life.

III. INDUSTRY.

He was a hard worker all his life. When aged more than three score years and ten, his labors put many a young man to the blush. In the days of his prime there seemed to be no end to his power of endurance. On one day he delivered ten addresses, and during the last seemed as fresh as if it were the first. In preparing a circular or report, he sometimes revised it twenty times before allowing it to be printed. His success resulted from patient, intelligent and persistent hard work. If he possessed genius, it was a genius for intense protracted application. Life was real and earnest to him, and he could never understand how an intelligent being could spend time in lounging and idleness. He had a poor opinion of drones, whether in or out of the Church; believing there was enough unemployed talent in the Church to evangelize the world.

He sometimes told with keen relish the story of Daniel Webster and his brother. When they were boys, their father told them one morning to mow some hay in the meadow. He then left them. The day was warm, and the boys preferred lounging to mowing. When their father returned at noon they had not mowed a stroke. He turned to the older boy and said, " Zeke, what have you been doing all the morning ?"

" Nothing, sir," was the reply.

Then putting the same question to Daniel, the reply was, "I have been helping Zeke, sir."

The Zekes and Daniels in the Church are retarding its prosperity.

CHAPTER XIX.

It is difficult to form an estimate of the influence and far-reaching results of such a life as Mr. McCullagh's. Having commenced his Sunday-school efforts in Great Britain, he worked as a volunteer missionary for seven years in the United States. Then he labored as a commissioned missionary of The American Sunday-School Union for eleven years. In 1852, in addition to his own missionary efforts, he was appointed to superintend the society's work in Kentucky and Tennessee. His territory was extended until, in 1867, he superintended the work in Virginia, Kentucky, Tennessee, North Carolina, South Carolina, Georgia, Alabama, Mississippi, Louisiana, Arkansas, Texas and Florida. Subsequently the three states lying west of the Mississippi river were transferred to the southwestern district. He continued to superintend the work in the remaining states until 1884, when, owing to the infirmities of age, he resigned the office of superintendent. Then he was commissioned as a general missionary, in which capacity he continued in the work until his death. Thus his connection with The American Sunday-School Union, as a volunteer, a commissioned missionary, superintendent and general missionary, extended over a period of fifty-four years.

During that time he organized 1000 Sunday-schools, containing 66,200 teachers and scholars. The subsequent growth and influence of these schools cannot be estimated. A goodly portion of them have grown into churches; and many of the scholars "found him, of whom Moses in the law, and the prophets, did write, Jesus of Nazareth."

His influence extended much farther than the schools that he organized personally. For more than thirty-six years an important part of his work was to collect money to support missionaries. As far back as 1857 we find that he raised over three thousand dollars a year—a sum sufficient to support five missionaries. This amount increased until, in 1866, his average collections were more than five thousand dollars per year. The entire sum of money that he raised for the missionary work by personal solicitation, through legacies and other sources, amounted to hundreds of thousands of dollars. What share of the credit for inducing God's people to contribute to this cause, and for the great work which the missionaries were thereby enabled to accomplish, should be accorded to him, we do not undertake to say.

During the years from 1867 to 1884, while he was superintendent of the southern district, 6459 new Sunday-schools were organized in that field, containing 304,000 teachers and scholars. Aid was rendered in 12,000 other cases to neighborhoods representing 638,700 teachers and scholars; 25,800 addresses were delivered; 82,400 Bibles and Testaments were distributed; and 63,400 families visited. It would be difficult to estimate the influence he exerted by wisely training the new missionaries placed under his care, and by cheering and encouraging them when discouraged.

What the harvest shall be from the good seed which he scattered in the Bibles, the many Sunday-school libraries, and the ten thousand volumes of good books he distributed, will be known only in the great day.

The number of Sunday-school scholars and young people whom he addressed could be numbered by the hundred thousand. What lasting impressions were made upon their young hearts, what resolutions were formed to hate sin and seek righteousness and the increase of Christian effort, are pleasant themes to consider.

What has been the result of his faithful words in the thousands of families that he visited and faithful admonitions by the wayside, we shall never know in this world. These suggestions are made to furnish suitable topics for contemplating the extent of such a work.

It is impossible to represent in figures the results of a well-spent life. A man's influence, be it for good or evil, lives after him. And it is a truth full of comfort to Christian people that God often honors their influence to accomplish more for his glory after their death, than they were permitted to see during their lives.

."Though scoffers ask, 'Where is your gain?'
　And mocking say, 'Your work is vain,'
　Such scoffers die and are forgot;
　Work done for God, it dieth not.

"Work on, work on, nor doubt nor fear.
　From age to age this voice shall cheer;
　Whate'er may die and be forgot,
　Work done for God, it dieth not."

A RETROSPECT.

Let us glance at the salient points of this history :

1. We learn the great importance of early religious training. That good Scotchwoman, his mother, but little realized what a valiant soldier of the cross she was training for battle, and the victories he would achieve on another continent.

2. We see the hand of Providence in human affairs. "The steps of a good man are ordered by the Lord." "I will guide thee with mine eye." He was bereaved of his family that he might become a son of consolation to thousands. His worldly possessions were swept away that he might make many know of "the depth of the riches, both of the wisdom and

knowledge of God." The cupidity of the ship agents prevented him from sailing on the "Margaret" that he might be the instrument, under God, of turning many from the way which leads to eternal death. He was preserved from the dangers of war that he might tell many of the peace of God which passeth all understanding.

3. We note all through his life the glorious efficacy of the gospel according to the promise, God's word shall not return unto him void. Let it be proclaimed even in the midst of ignorance and vice and the results are astonishing. It is still the power of God unto salvation, and, as a practical working power, demonstrates its strength when subjected to the severest tests.

4. We perceive the value and need of Christian heroism; that the dauntless, intrepid soldiers of the cross who invade the enemies' territory can win imperishable laurels.

5. We perceive the importance of continuing this foundation work to which his life was devoted. Vice, ignorance and crime are of rapid growth. A large percentage of the inmates of

our prisons are boys and young men. Corrupt and infidel literature is being scattered broadcast to contaminate the young. There are many thousands of dark places without the Sunday-school or church. There are still from eight to ten millions of children and youth in our country who are not receiving moral and religious training. From their wide distribution, and from the choice and preference of the people in these destitute places, it seems as if the hand of Providence points to united Christian effort as the available and effectual means of gathering them for religious instruction.

CLOSING YEARS.

In March, 1884, Mr. McCullagh, being seventy-three years of age, his hearing having almost entirely failed, and being greatly afflicted with rheumatism, asked to be relieved of his duties as superintendent.

He had always looked forward to a quiet and peaceful old age, in which he could spend his time at home, free from the anxieties and battles of life. He remarked, "When a man who has toiled all of his days reaches the age of seventy years, he should spend the short remaining time as a kind of sabbatical period, in closing up his earthly affairs, and in making special preparation for his eternal rest."

After a few months, however, his health greatly improved, and his time, as general missionary, was spent in advancing the work with his pen. He contributed a number of articles to *The Sunday-School World*, wrote missionary letters to the patrons of the society, and continued his correspondence with all of his co-laborers in the Sunday-school work.

On account of deafness, he was cut off from social intercourse with his neighbors and friends. He spent much time in reading. When fatigued from reading and writing, his garden afforded him an endless source of diversion and relaxation. Trimming his trees and raspberries, training grapevines, working in the strawberry bed and among vegetables, experimenting with various methods of gardening, were duties followed with unflagging interest. From such careful cultivation the yield of his garden was astonishing. Every tree and plant he watched as closely as a mother would her child.

During his last years he was frequently called to mourn the loss of some dear personal friend or relative. It was owing to his extensive acquaintance, both North and South, that these sad announcements were so often received. "I feel like an old tree standing alone," he said; "my friends and co-laborers are falling on every side. It will soon be my time; this old body can't stand much longer." While deeply depressed at the death of his friends, his usual frame of mind was bright and cheerful.

He took as much interest and pleasure in life as a young person. There was nothing morbid or gloomy in his views of life or death. When asked how long he would like to live, he replied, "I am ready whenever my time comes; but if left to me, to live just one day longer than Methuselah would suit me very well." He became more patient, gentle and trustful as the years passed by, and spent much time in reading the Scriptures and devotional books. His humility was beautiful and touching; he never regarded anything that he had done as a ground for his personal acceptance with God.

"It is all of grace. The great sacrifice that was once offered is complete in every respect. The atoning blood of Christ cleanseth from all sin. I trust not my own merits, but in his finished righteousness."

Owing to deafness, he was in his later years debarred the pleasure of attending public worship. His anxiety to hear some part of the service was such a strain upon his nervous system that it produced an intense pain in his head. The last sermon that he heard was from Dr. B. M. Palmer, of New Orleans. "Every thing that liveth, which moveth, whithersoever the rivers shall come, shall live" (Ezekiel 47 : 9).

The discourse depicted the glory and life-giving power of the gospel; like a mighty stream with its banks covered with verdure and flowers, it carried life and blessing wherever it flows; so the gospel carries not only life but eternal life. The first sermon that he heard in America was from the text "Ye are my witnesses, saith the Lord." By the blessing of God he became a faithful witness. The last was a description of that eternal life which the gospel imparts, and was a fitting close of the great subject.

The last contribution that he made was to help build a little Sunday-school room in the suburbs of Henderson. Forty-nine years before he had raised the Sunday-school banner in this part of Kentucky, and almost with his dying hands aided in keeping that banner waving. Thus he left off where he began, his first and last effort being for Sunday-schools.

On Saturday, August 18, 1888, he read at family worship, with great emotion, the last chapter of the Revelation. That day he wrote his last two letters; one to Missionary Forster, thanking him for a walking-cane he had kindly sent him; the other to Mr. Peter Lott, a contributor in New York.

On Sunday, August 19, he complained of a slight dizziness in his head. He retired early at night, and, according to his custom, prayed aloud when going to his room. A short time after, he made an effort to call the family. When we reached him he was unconscious, and passed away quietly and sweetly, without a struggle.

An artery in the brain had parted, and earth's trials ended. The Master called, and his spirit obeyed.

> "Yet speaketh! Though the voice is hushed that filled
>   Cathedral nave or choir, like clearest bell,
>   With music of God's truth,—that softly thrilled
>   The silence of the mourner's heart—that fell
>   So sweetly, oh so sweetly, on the ears
>   Of those to whom that voice was dearest of the dear.
>
> "Yet speaketh! There was no last word of love,
>   So suddenly on us the sorrow fell;
>   His bright translation to the home above
>   Was clouded with no shadow of farewell;
>   His final evening closed with praise and prayer,
>   And then began the songs of joy up there.
>
> "Yet speaketh! O my father, now more dear
>   Than ever, I have cried—oh speak to me
>   Only once more, once more!   But now I hear
>   The far-off whisper of sweet melody:
>   Thou art yet speaking on the heavenly hill,
>   Each word a note of joy—and shall we not be still?"

He had requested that but one inscription be put on his monument: "With long life will I satisfy him, and show him my salvation." Loving hands laid him away to rest in the beautiful valley of the Ohio, where he had valiantly fought the good fight of faith.   Here he sleeps sweetly until the resurrection of the just. Here he shall rest until he sees the morning break on the golden shore.

"And I heard a voice from heaven, saying unto me, Write, Blessed *are* the dead which die in the Lord from henceforth: Yea, saith the Spirit, that they may rest from their labours; and their works do follow them."

CHAPTER XX.

VIEWS OF HIS CHARACTER.

AFTER Mr. McCullagh had passed away, a multitude of letters were received from all parts of the Union, expressing the love and esteem with which he was regarded. The following extracts have been selected as representing the sentiments of them all.

The Rev. James M. Crowell, D.D., Secretary of Missions of The American Sunday-School Union, wrote:

"His life-work was a magnificent record of faithful toil and valiant service for the Lord and Master whom he so ardently loved. And surely the history of The American Sunday-School Union is crowded with facts and incidents associated with his good work. How dearly he loved our society and the children and their Saviour."

The Rev. H. Clay Trumbull, D.D., editor of *The Sunday-School Times*, said:

"Delightful memories of my experience with

your dear father come back to me as I learn that he has finally entered into rest. I am glad of the life he lived; I cannot be sorry for the death he died. I sympathize with you in the personal loss of his taking away; I rejoice with you in memory of his loving service for his Master and in the assured hope of his presence with the Lord."

A. G. Adams, of Nashville, wrote:

"From his pious and consistent and devoted life, his end was just what our Lord has promised."

Colonel Bennett H. Young, president of the Louisville Southern Railroad Company, writes to the son:

"I have often said, I would rather have your father's crown in glory than any man's I had ever known. Many may have excelled him in many things, but none have brought more souls to Christ, and none lived more consecrated lives. You have already appropriated the promises and comforts of the gospel. You are indeed rich in the assurance of having a father so full of good works and faith, and one who did such valiant service for Jesus."

The Rev. G. S. Jones, of Hendersonville, N. C., for many years a missionary of the Union in Mr. McCullagh's district, says:

"Yours of the 23d inst. brings me such news as makes me feel like stepping softly. A sense of sadness takes possession of my soul. I look again over the last letter written me by your dear father, and, laying it down, ask myself, is it possible I am no more to be thus greeted? Ah, my prayer is, Lord, let the spirit of devotion to the great work in which John McCullagh lived and labored abide on me, even me, till at the appointed time I, too, shall quietly exchange the cross for the crown. In a wreath of deathless memories the name of McCullagh will hold a century's union with our good old society that cares for the children."

The Rev. Isaac Emory, of Knoxville, Tenn., another experienced missionary, writes:

"It is twenty-two years this month since I first met with him at Nashville, and at his earnest solicitation consented to come to East Tennessee, and received my commission from The American Sunday-School Union. I said I would enter the service for five years, provided the Lord blessed me in my work; but he said it must be for life—that he had thus enlisted. He has been to me a spiritual father, dearly beloved. Sometimes, when weary in my work, but never of it, he would cheer me with the words of Luther, 'Work on earth and rest in heaven.' Now he has entered into that rest."

Howard W. Hunter, of Louisville, Ky., says:

"The sympathies of many hearts in our school (as indeed over many states) are with you; while we cannot but rejoice that the battle-scarred veteran of many battles has laid off his armor to receive the laurel wreath of victory. Oh how blessed is such a death! When we contemplate his reward, how ought we to be incited to acts of heroism and of self-denial! What an immense circle of friends he has 'up there'!"

Rev. W. P. Paxson, D.D., superintendent of the southwestern district, writes:

"It was my privilege to be closely connected with Brother McCullagh in several of our extended eastern trips in behalf of the cause he so dearly loved, and I learned to love him next to my own father; and I mourn his loss. Yet why mourn? His life's labor was done and well done, and he has gone to meet the rest of that noble band of veterans who have gone on before. May the Lord give us, who succeed to the labors of such men, the wisdom and grace to be as faithful and efficient!"

L. Milton Marsh, secretary at New York, writes:

"His was a long, useful, blessed life. How truly can it be said of him, 'He hath done what he could'! Very few pastors have been permitted to preach Christ to as many souls as he."

R. G. Chisolm, of Charleston, a vice-president of the society, writes of Mr. McCullagh:

"A long life well spent; a battle nobly won; and the end peace and joy."

Hon. John W. Simonton, of Harrisburg, Pa., writes:

"Your honored father did a great work for the Master; and while he rests from his labors his works will follow him."

James P. Orr, of Pittsburgh, Pa., says:

"Mr. McCullagh's life and work was a grand

success; far more so than the success that the world applauds. He had treasure laid up in heaven. It is a great comfort to know that he has gone to a sure reward. We have lost a friend here, and gained one in the throng beyond."

Rev. Edwin W. Rice, D.D., editor of The American Sunday-School Union, from his summer vacation of rest by the sea-side wrote:

"If I was counted among his intimate friends by your father it was because he was ever a true, manly and Christian friend to me. How kindly he took me by the hand and taught me how to reach the hearts and to some extent the 'purses' of the people, when I was 'fresh' and a poor scholar in such business in the West. I remember with sincere reverence his gentle and firm teaching. What a great gap he has left among our forces! That splendid band of veterans are fast passing away! I begin to feel lonely! There were Tousley, Corey, Stephen Paxson, McCullagh, Chidlaw and others; noble men all of them; each a peer in his place; and of them all, no man could wield the influence in the South and the North, and could reach the 'pockets' of the people, by public and personal appeals, in as effective and pleasant a manner as dear old John McCullagh. He was always sure to win a man by a personal interview; he would gain him as a 'friend to the cause,' even if he received no contribution on the first application.   In this work he was *facile princeps*; his tact, persuasive power, sweetness of temper in rebuffs, and endless patience, perseverance and dead earnestness, carried everything and everybody before him. . . . The great desire of his heart, 'to die in the harness' and to pass away peacefully and without great pain, was graciously answered of the Lord."

The *Presbyterian Banner*, noticing his death, adds :

" Mr. McCullagh was known far and wide throughout the land as the children's preacher and indefatigable Sunday-school worker.   For more than half a century he was identified with the great work of The American Sunday-School Union.   He was one of the grand pioneer laborers for this cause in the Ohio valley. Through his efforts thousands of Sunday-schools have been organized, and tens of thousands of children have learned the sweet story of Jesus and his love. After a three minutes' encounter with death, the veteran toiler passed into the presence of his Lord and King to behold his glory and beauty."

The *Sunday-School World* closed an extended notice of Mr. McCullagh's life with these appreciative words :

" When the battle of earth had been fought, without pain or sickness Mr. McCullagh rested from his labors August 20, 1888, at the age of nearly seventy-seven. His works follow him and his memory is blessed. His earnest enthusiasm, his untiring energy and his good judgment of men rendered him a very efficient superintendent of the missionary work in the South. His relations with the home office in Philadelphia were always of the most pleasant character. His affection for the society continued to be most ardent to the end of life. The officers and managers always commended his zeal, and confided in his good judgment as a most valuable and energetic co-worker with themselves in the great work of caring for the neglected children of the land."

The *Christian Observer*, of Louisville, Ky., after referring to his death, adds :

" For a long time he has been the agent of The American Sunday-School Union, and as such he visited many of our congregations. His advent was always welcomed, for the ' Old Missionary' would not fail to bring with him a cheery face and a happy word for all. Age did not seem to mar the brightness of his smile or the cordiality of his manner. The illustrations that he used in talking with the schools were always pertinent and effective. . . . He came to Kentucky nearly fifty years ago, and has made his home at Henderson, we think, continuously ever since. Some time ago his health failed, and he has been calmly awaiting the call of the Master to enter into the rest that is reserved for all those that love his appearing."

The *Courier-Journal*, of Louisville, Ky., announced his death and adds :

" He was well known throughout the South, having for a number of years occupied the position of superintendent of The American Sunday-School Union for the southern district. Mr. McCullagh was a truly good man and respected citizen. His loss is mourned by the whole community."

The *Henderson Journal* gave an extended notice of his work in founding a church at that place and of his wider labors in the South, closing thus:

"Sufficient to say that the thousands of Sunday-schools established through his agency, and the tens of thousands of children brought to a knowledge of the light and truth by his means, are monuments of which any man might be proud."

The *Henderson News* gives an interesting picture of his home-life and character:

"No citizen of Henderson has been more honorably mentioned by its press, after death, than has been Rev. John McCullagh.

"Like a weary pilgrim who had journeyed far, he came to the river's brink, where he laid down his burdens and prepared to cross to the farther side. He had worked during the allotted three score and ten; and although he was 'living on borrowed time,' as he sometimes expressed it, his intellect was not allowed to rest in idleness, nor the feeble hands to rest from their labors.

"Always a toiler in his Master's vineyard while health and strength permitted, his interest in the cause and the Church never flagged to the last. Unlike most persons who engage in literary or public work of any kind, in spite of the engrossing cares of his vocation, he had always time and sympathy for the discharge, in detail, of the duties devolving upon him as a husband or father. Whether his counsel was needed in the solution of a knotty problem in a business enterprise, or to soothe the schoolboy woes of a little grandchild, each one turned to him, and none failed in obtaining the desired aid and sympathy. Although an alien from the home of his birth, he identified himself with the interests of his adopted land, and was ever a faithful and worthy citizen. He grappled with the difficulties of adverse fortune, and bore off spoils where weaker natures would have yielded to despair. But the rewards of his diligence and persevering energy were never consumed in self-indulgence, as he was ever frugal to himself. To the cause of Christianity the first fruits of his success were always devoted, and afterwards his family and friends came in for a generous share.

" Endowed himself with a fine intellect, great powers of endurance, strength of purpose, unusual fortitude and force of character, united with tender affections and unswerving religious sentiments, he transmitted to his offspring and nurtured in them the same noble traits.

" ' Ye shall know them by their fruits.'

"A hero indeed he must have been to those associated with him in the daily walks of life, when such were the impressions made by his life upon one who only caught the glimmer of his taper from afar as it flitted on the way.

'Over the river they beckon to me—
    Loved ones long gone to the farther side;
The gleam of their snowy robes I see,
    But their voices are drowned in the rushing tide.
You see not the angels waiting there,
    The gates of the city you cannot see;
Over the river—the peaceful river—
    Loved ones are waiting to welcome me.

'I've watched for a gleam of the flapping sail—
    I hear the boat as it gains the strand;
I shall pass from sight with the boatman pale
    To the better shore of the spirit-land.
I shall know the loved who have gone before,
    And joyfully sweet will the meeting be,
When over the river—the peaceful river—
    The Angel of Death has carried me.' "

www.ingramcontent.com/pod-product-compliance
Lightning Source LLC
Chambersburg PA
CBHW031109020726
47495CB00007B/2110